THAT'S ALL
I KNOW

THAT'S ALL
I KNOW

Elisa Levi

Translated from the Spanish by Christina MacSweeney

DAUNT BOOKS

This edition first published in the United Kingdom in 2025 by
Daunt Books
83 Marylebone High Street
London W1U 4QW

1

Copyright © Elisa Levi, 2021

English translation copyright © Christina MacSweeney, 2025

First published in Spain by Ediciones Temas de Hoy as
Yo No Soy de Otras Cosas

The right of Elisa Levi to be identified as author of this work
has been asserted by her in accordance with the Copyright,
Designs and Patents Act 1988

The right of Christina MacSweeney to be identified as
translator of this work has been asserted by her in accordance
with the Copyright, Designs and Patents Act 1988

[grant wording TK]

A CIP catalogue record for this title
is available from the British Library.

ISBN 978-1-914198-78-6

Typeset by Marsha Swan
Printed and bound by TJ Books Limited, Padstow, Cornwall

www.dauntbookspublishing.co.uk

THAT'S ALL
I KNOW

RUMINATING, LIKE COWS DO

I tell the man that the only thing he'll find on this path is forest. That's all I know. 'But it's in there,' he replies. No, no, no way, I insist. You'll die if you go into the forest. If you want, I'll point the way or take you to where your dog is. 'You don't need to do that,' he says. And I say, 'Around here, dogs that haven't eaten always go to the same place.' 'But my dog's in there,' he repeats. No, no, no way. I put a hand out to stop him 'cause I know that people who go into the forest never come out. They never reach anywhere and they die. They get tired and dehydrated. Or they get tired and die of cold. Or they get tired and life no longer offers them a way forward. I tug on his arm and explain. I explain that I belong here more than anyone else, that I might not be very old, but I know this place 'cause I have a backstory. I say that if he wants, I'll tell him my story: I lost a dog when I was younger and it was with the hares.

You're from goodness knows where, so you don't know this, but around here lost dogs follow the scent of food and their frantic owners go rushing into the forest. I can't count the number of people I've seen never return from the Landas, from the woodlands. You don't know the first thing about it, but the fact is there's no way out of that forest. And I notice that the man's breathing sounds laboured and the beads of sweat falling from his brow could fill every well for miles around. The expression on his face moves me, makes me think I could tell him all about it. I could tell him that I'm leaving, that I've decided to leave this small place. And I soon begin to think this lost, confused man is the only person in the world who might understand me. Yes, he, and he alone, might understand me.

You see, I say, sitting him down to rest on the bench I'm leaning against; this bench is always in the shade and if the man goes on sweating like that, he'll die without ever finding his dog. You see, I say, my dog got lost one Sunday in summer and my sister – she's empty-headed 'cause she didn't breathe when she was being born – cried in a different way. Nora usually only cries when her body hurts her. If you pinch her, she cries, if her stomach

4

rumbles, she cries. But love, loneliness, sorrow; none of those things makes her cry. And that summer morning she cried 'cause the dog didn't come back and our father said, 'It's gone to the place where the dead hares are.' And, would you believe it, Nora cried less. Around here, there are piles of dead hares. Animals that die lie in a heap and make an awful stink. But then, sir, I don't know anything about stinks 'cause I've never had a sense of smell, just like my mother, though she says she could smell a little as a teenager, but I've never been able to. And that's a pity 'cause they say the scent of our tomatoes carries for miles. But that's all I know about smells, and you don't know anything about dogs that get lost here. We know about other things. Anyway, when we got there, the dog was dead. And my mother saw the blood dripping from its jaws and cried out, 'It must have been a wolf.'

But I knew it had been Esteban – he lives across from where the hares are piled up – he's sort of trigger-happy and we don't get many wolves in these parts. Esteban went and killed my dog, and I wanted to kill him for making my sister cry. But don't you worry, just sit here quietly, your dog is filling its stomach and we'll see it sniffing around here again soon. Dogs aren't like me, I can tell you. I'm more like a cat; they sniff and come to care for you. Just rest here with me, your shirt is all soaked in sweat. You'll see, the dog will soon turn up.

The man and I sit, looking into the forest, and I note how he's sweating. If you're hot, you can take your shirt off, your dog might take its time coming back, I say. I just need to rest here awhile, he replies, then I'll go in there to look for him. No, no, no way, I tell him, really, don't insist, don't be fooled by my baby face, I'm fully nineteen years old and I know that when people go into the woodlands, darkness falls on them. This forest is treacherous, like the river when it's flowing fast. There are no paths in this part of the woodlands and the firebreak is a long way off. The old folk say that if you go right across it, you'll reach the sea, though I don't believe them. But then I don't understand north, south, east and west. I know about other things. Here, people look at the moss to figure out which way is which or they remember where the sun and the moon come up. As for me, the sun's always catching me off guard, sometimes on my left, sometimes on my right. The forest is dangerous. Not even the civil guard go looking for people who get lost there 'cause they don't want to go into the Landas, and we have no forest rangers here; we're so remote nobody is interested. Mother Nature made the forest for us to be frightened of, so death, despair, and darkness would always be in our minds, 'cause when you go in there you can't see the sun, there's only dark shadows, and no matter how much moss, how many compasses, how good a sense of

6

direction or memory you have, the forest gobbles you up like a hungry rabbit.

You'll leave your dog an orphan if you don't listen to me, sir. The man takes off his shirt and heat wafts from his skin. His body is wrinkly, but I figure he must be still in his sixties. He takes out his mobile phone and makes a grumbling noise in his throat. There's practically no coverage in town; there is in Pueblo Grande, but here the signal gets lost. Like I said, this is the world's end.

I hope you don't mind if I smoke, I say, but the man neither looks at me nor responds. I can let you have some if you like; it's the tobacco mixed with a little weed that Marco left at my door last night. He does that from time to time, and I like to come here to smoke it 'cause when I smoke Marco's weed and stare into the forest, I imagine that the woodlands don't exist and so I can see everything on the other side. But the man says nothing and doesn't even look at me.

It's hot for January, isn't it? I say. And he agrees that it's hot for January.

In this green, leafy town, the sun doesn't bring anyone out into the street, I tell him. Except for Juana, who's still mourning her brother and, when I go to get bread, I take some for her 'cause she eats so little these days. And what I usually say to her is, 'Juana, it's always darkest before the dawn.' I can't tell you how it hurts to see her out there, sitting alone, next to her brother's empty chair. 'Juana,' I shout merrily when I see her, 'time cures everything except old age and madness.' And she laughs. And I leave the bread on her brother's empty chair so she knows that death is just one day, not a whole life, and where her brother once sat there's now bread, and that's that.

The man turns to look at me and I say that I might be young, but I already know that's how death is. When a person dies, they don't take happiness with them, I say. The dead don't take anything with them; death is just four tears and a pain in your breast, but life goes on for those of us left behind. And just as soon as the tears leave your eyes, they turn into water. And the man laughs, but I think that's 'cause he doesn't want to think of death that way. This man doesn't have the first idea. You don't know where you've ended up, I say, you know nothing about this town. Let me explain, we have plenty of time; if you stay here with me, your dog will return sooner or later. Dogs always come back. But you wouldn't know that. And the man looks at me, but I look into the forest.

The man is sweating like a pig that's about to slaughtered.

I don't have any water with me, sir, I say, but if you want, you can rest your head on my shoulder. Javier often does. Put his head on my shoulder, I mean. And sometimes

I touch his face when he does that. But I won't touch yours. In town they say I'm a chatterbox, and I talk even more when I smoke Marco's weed. But maybe, now that you have plenty of time, you won't mind listening to me.

Not many people come here. And the man's breathing speeds up. Were you aware of that, or is it another thing you don't know? And the man looks at me and says that he doesn't really know how he ended up here, on the edge of this small town. You got lost with your dog and now your dog's lost you. Don't worry, that sort of thing happens to people who are new to the area.

And what are you doing here? the man asks. Waiting, I reply. I'm waiting with you for your lost dog. The man sighs and I'm sure he's sighing 'cause it's always better to wait with someone else. If you get lost again tomorrow, you won't find me here. What am I doing here, waiting quietly in the shade? I'm waiting for your dog and ruminating, chewing the cud, like cows do, sir. I'm ruminating about everything I plan to do tomorrow. Listen, how about I wait here with you for your dog and you keep me company on this strange afternoon of the first day of the year? And I look at the man, but he's looking into the forest.

I don't know what kind of life you've had or how you felt when you woke this morning, but when I woke my gut was burning. It burned and burned the way the

9

undergrowth burns in this weird January heat. But don't go thinking this is the first time I've felt fire in my gut. And don't even think of saying it's the weed making my gut burn. My gut has been burning for a while, but this morning, when I woke, I understood why. I'm chewing the cud, sir, ruminating about what I'm going to do tomorrow.

If Javier was sitting here with us, sir, he'd call you an elf 'cause you don't know anything about this place, and that's Javier's name for people who pass through this world's end. And elves never hang around, they always leave or disappear. I like Javier 'cause I'm attracted to men who aren't sad the whole time. As for you, I tell the man, looking at the bags under his eyes and his crow's feet; you haven't smiled even once, you have a lot of sadness about you. Javier, on the other hand, is always smiling. Whenever he comes into my mother's grocery store, he brightens up my morning and I say to the customers, 'Here comes the handsome guy I love and who loves me.' And they answer, 'The swan envies the ugly duckling's luck.' And I laugh and laugh, and sometimes I even sing, and when my mother comes to help me serve, she says, 'You won't always have something to sing about.' But I insist, 'Dance, Ma, you never dance at home these days.' And my mother says, 'If only I was as young as you, Little Lea' – here in town, we're known as Big Lea and Little Lea. And I call out happily, 'If only the little one has the big one's luck.' But deep down, I've never wanted my mother's luck. I mean, I want to see the world, find a job in the city. And earn money and spend it on the things everyone else does: plans, after-school classes for my future daughter, holidays abroad, technology. I want to live on an island, an island without forests, with hardly any plants, almost a desert island, but with opportunities. And one day I want to tell the daughter, 'That's enough. You spend all day glued to that screen.' The things I know can be useful in other places too, right?

When the heat gets suffocating, not a soul walks along the dusty streets of this town, and that's why it's smart of you to wait with me here. Do you have children? You don't look like you do. The man turns to me and smiles. No, you don't have any children. I thought so. If I have a daughter one day, I won't let her get to know rabbits. I'll let her milk cows; when you milk you learn to be grateful. Grateful to animals, not to God and all those lies. But she'll know nothing about rabbits 'cause there's no need for her to experience how bitter life can be, at least not while I'm caring for her. And what's more, my daughter will be born in the city and will have processed food, 'cause that's what city kids eat, and I – a city mother – will complain and at PTA meetings, I'll ask them to change the menu in the cafeteria, tell them that since I come from a small town, I know your lifespan is related to your diet.

But believe it or not, all that would be roleplaying, like an actor, 'cause I'm not interested in my daughter having a long life; at a certain age, life gets incomprehensible. You only have to look at the old folk in this town; they don't understand the first thing. I'm ruminating, sir, 'cause my gut is burning. And the man looks at me, but I'm looking into the forest.

Forgive me if I sometimes talk too fast, but there's a kind of pressure in my chest that makes the words speed up, and the heat makes my mouth dry too. My mother says the heat is due to all the stuff cars spew out; she says cars are iniquities, along with the forest and spiritual ailments. If I worked at the town hall, I'd ban cars. Don't be so naïve, the neighbours sometimes tell me, your hands are more valuable here. But I know that my most valuable asset is my head 'cause once, when a television crew turned up to make a documentary for the regional channel, I looked straight at the camera and spoke out, convinced of what I was saying. The kid told me that if it came out well, they'd send it to the national – I don't know if it came out well 'cause when it was supposed to be broadcast, we had violent storms that left us cut off for a month. Anyway, when the TV people arrived, they asked me and Catalina some questions; she didn't open her mouth, but I talked about the things we needed. My head is a real asset 'cause I'm a fast thinker and I know how make use of the moment. So I said we needed money for a proper walk-in clinic 'cause there are so many old folk here and the doctor only comes once every two weeks. And I also said we needed better public transport, said there were only two buses a day. And I begged them to repair the regional highway and give us a direct bus route to the coast; though we're so near the sea, you can take it from me that it's the tourists who get all the benefits! The sea belongs to us more than anyone else! The kid from the video said the documentary was called *Empty New Spain* and, looking straight at the camera, the way actors do, I said no way was it empty, they only had to look to notice we're alive and kicking. I said empty was the natural condition of the forest, but Spain was still very full here. But I forgave the kid when he said I looked like this actress, an actress from somewhere else. He told me where, but I don't know anything about the names of other places. Then I made a last-minute addition to my list of requests, one that later made Javier laugh. This year, I said, at the summer festival, I want a group to come and sing that song that goes, 'I'm nothing without you, a rain-drop wetting my face'. Javier laughed and laughed some more and wondered what had come over me to say that. And I said it was a present for him 'cause the first time I told him I thought he was attractive, that song was playing in the background.

But that's not what I want to tell you about. What I really want to tell you is why, if your dog were to get lost tomorrow, you wouldn't find me here in the shade. Has your life ever got tangled? Well, mine has. It's got into a knot that I don't know how to untie. I'm ruminating about what to do tomorrow, sir. Life in this town is going to drag on and when your gut complains it's 'cause there's a decision to be made. When I ask the man if he believes in the end of the world, he closes his eyes to laugh. And his laughter rings out, booms in my ears, and I laugh too, but that's 'cause I'm always ready to laugh. Yes, yes, I mean it, I say. And the man dries the tears from his eyes with his shirt. Have you seen the black ribbons in the windows of all the houses in town? They're for the end of the world, sir.

Last year, when my mother opened the store on January the first, all the locals swarmed in like flies around a horse's muzzle. They were upset, sir, coming and going like crazy. And my mother overheard what they were talking about. 'It seems the world is going to end this year,' she told me, and I laughed, just like you did, and said, 'They're running out of things to invent in town!' But my mother looked all doubtful, so I cheerfully added, 'Ma, you don't believe that, it's the sort of thing they make up in other places. We're so remote here even the end of the world would forget to include us.' But as I said that, my gut started to burn for the first time. And now, a year later, it's burning just as hard, like some madman had set fire to his own land. But then, the next day Catalina came by and while I was cleaning the yard where the hens live, she asked if I'd heard the talk about the end of the world and I said I had, but told her that foolish words fall on deaf ears. And my gut was churning again. She stood there, thinking, and I said we should wait and see what they were saying in Pueblo Grande 'cause the internet isn't much use here. We did find some stuff about the Mayan Calendar, but I knew straight off there was no truth in it; just some ridiculous made-up story, but people were starting to feel scared and talked of nothing else.

In small places, sir, people need to believe in something just to fill their days. And there came the day when a neighbour said it was true, that in other countries, far, far away, they believed it so firmly that the inhabitants were losing their minds. And then one morning another man told us that his daughter – the one who lives in the capital – had said there were rumours there too. And a woman came in the next day and told us she'd read in the newspaper that, in fact, someone or other had predicted it in the past and people who knew about such things were saying that this year would see the end of everything. And yet another day, Juana turned up and said she hoped beyond hope it was true, that she wanted it all to end so she could choose to be dead, like her brother. And then another neighbour said his cows were beginning to act strange and another said his dogs were howling at the moon and that could only mean the world was reaching its end. And the local papers didn't help; they had headlines saying yes, yes, it's true, the world is ending. And then Esteban – the man who killed my dog – pointing his gun to the ground for the first time in his life, said it was too hot for January, and the rivers were running dry upstream and that could only be 'cause the end was coming. And the mayor – who's always first in line to back any conspiracy theory – decreed 2012 to be an official year of mourning. And whether they asked me or not, I told everyone, 'You don't know the first thing! The mayor just wants our minds taken up with foolish stuff like the end of the world so we don't bother him with complaints. The world isn't coming to an end; the only thing that's going to end is this town, unless we start to stand up for ourselves.'

I suppose you'd have said the same. But, anyway, after that life started to tighten the noose and a fire settled in my gut. I don't know, I really don't know if it's just my whole world that's been killing itself this last year, or if the world only came to an end here, in this small town. But the truth is that, all things considered, today, on the first day of a new year, I can firmly state that the world did end yesterday. And I'll tell you why.

The man puts on his shirt and gets to his feet. Don't go, I say – I feel like crying, but I don't tell him that. Stay a while longer, I know where your dog is and, truly, we just have to wait. I promise. I swear. You're staring at me, staring at me, don't stare at me that way, I say. If you stay here, the dog will turn up. You're staring at me, staring at me, don't stare at me that way—but I don't say that. And he sits down again 'cause he knows nothing about this place, and right now, on this first afternoon of the new year, with ribbons hanging in the windows of the houses behind us, I'm the only person in the world the man has and he's the only person in the world I have.

I WAS WALKING ALONG
THE COBBLED STREET

It's definitely hot for January, but you wouldn't believe the heat we had last March, I tell the man. And what's more, in 2012 there was no rain, and the sun beat down like a curse. There are four young people living here in town: Javier, Catalina, Marco and me, and since we're so alone, we're almost always together. Well, yes, there's my sister Nora, sir, she's young too but, no, she doesn't count. Being born here has made us accomplices; I'm not sure in what, maybe in our own existence. You see, very little happens here and there's hardly anywhere to go and everyone knows that if you're not in one place, you'll be in another. That's why we like smoking Marco's weed, sir; 'cause even if the four of us are together, in the same space, sitting around the same table, when we smoke, each of us gets lost in the images in our own heads, and no one can find us there, and we can't even find ourselves.

Marco is like an oak tree with a stout trunk and aggressive, invasive, uncontrolled roots; that's how Marco is, sir. On the other hand, Javier is more like a slender strawberry tree that could almost be mistaken for a shrub, but with reddish fruit, like his cheeks when he's been in the sun or when the heat burns his shoulders. My mother has always told me that Madrid has a monopoly on strawberry trees, but the truth is that the climate isn't right for them there and that's why there are so few. Javier's like that, sir; he wouldn't survive in another climate, much as I'd like to take him somewhere else. Catalina is more like a mimosa tree. A mimosa tree that's missing a branch or has a twisted root that sets her off balance. The thing is that Catalina burned her leg and now has a scar that looks like a rough stone and a limp she's set on having operated. I'm always telling her not to bother, it won't solve anything. But she keeps saving and saving from what little she earns, and if she goes on, she'll be able to buy up the whole town by the time she's thirty. My sister, sir, is a plant all of her own, there's no need to compare her with other ones. And in spite of there being barely two hundred of us, we have a lot of old folks in this town. What we don't have here, the thing we have little experience with, is people who come from other places and stay. We don't know much about that, so when the March sun was beating down on my head and Catalina started telling me about Jimena's house, my stomach got as sore as when my mother came home to tell me about the end of the world.

I was walking down the cobbled street when I saw Catalina coming toward me. Jimena's house has been sold, she said. Jimena was my grandmother, sir, but my mother wouldn't have anything to do with her, she used to call her 'that woman', and when she died, my mother refused to accept the house and it became town property. I never called my grandmother 'grandma'. But Jimena did love me. Even if she didn't love Big Lea, she loved Little Lea, and that's why she used to leave me flowers at the stop where we waited for the school bus. At first Javier, Marco and Catalina laughed, saying they were from some old man I'd made fall for me. But I knew they were from Jimena; Jimena loved me, and those flowers used to hang in her windows. In exchange, I'd leave fruit from the store on her doormat, and whenever my mother caught me at it, she'd say, 'Always suspect the worst of people', and I'd answer, 'A good deed is never wasted'.

'And exactly who has sold the house? If it belongs to the town, who gets the money?' I asked Catalina. 'Pueblo Grande, I suppose,' she answered. If I were in charge of the district, I tell the man, that house would already be a walk-in clinic. Like I said, my most valuable asset is my head. 'They say the people who bought it are from the city,' said Catalina. 'Don't be silly. Who's going to leave the city by the sea to come to this town?' 'No, no, that's not it,' retorted Catalina, 'they're not from these parts, they've come from the centre, from Madrid, and they've got tired of the city and want some countryside, some forest.' 'They only want the forest 'cause they've never seen it close up,' I told Catalina.

If I were running this town, I'd have signs put up, sir, enormous billboards on poles dug into the ground, saying: What you're looking for isn't here. People don't realise it, but small towns smell of cow dung, and piles of dead animals, and fear, and resentment, and boredom, and sorrow, and hatreds that pass from one generation to the next. And people from other places fall in love with some weird idea of what it means to have to bear the emptiness of the countryside, the slow passage of the days.

Catalina went on, 'She's a painter and he's come to set up a creamery, making cheeses.' 'A creamery? Don't we already have plenty of cheese here?' I snapped in reply. 'They don't care about what we already have, plus they're bringing a young child.' 'How young?' 'Three, five, I don't know.' 'That child will get bored,' I told her and then asked, 'What are they going to do here?' 'The same as you and me, Lea. Live.' Live, she said. Live. And that's when my gut started burning again. And it was like acid bile rising up my throat.

Well, sir, as far as I know, something has to be put up for sale before you can buy it, and there had been no for-sale sign outside Jimena's house. I was boiling with rage 'cause my grandmother had a very lonely life in that house. And I don't know why she stayed closed up in there for such a long time; for almost twenty years, my grandmother only went out once a week to leave me flowers and buy groceries. And she bought very little; she was so thin that if you looked at her side on, you could miss her. My grandmother died alone in her bed and it was the neighbours who held the vigil 'cause my mother never got over her anger. I don't know what my grandmother did that was so unforgivable, but it doesn't bother me 'cause even though hatred is inherited in small towns – the way cows and businesses are – none of that hate was ever passed on to me. Jimena's house is one of the largest in town, by a long shot. And the reason is that when she was newly wed, she thought about the future and imagined herself with a large extended family, but life only gave her one daughter and a husband who died young, and she was left alone, passing her days in a house that was too big, in a town that was too small. You won't believe it, sir, but my grandfather only took her to the coast once; in her whole life she saw the sea a total of five times. 'It's truly sad,' I'd say to my mother, 'to be so near the water, but to only ever see the forest.' And my mother would answer, 'What you can't see doesn't exist, Lea.' Ma stopped seeing my grandmother and my grandmother stopped existing. If she was alive now, I'd put Jimena in the car and take her to the sea; I'd spend money and we'd pick a hotel with hammocks on the shoreline. But I was too young to do that back then.

I left Catalina there and went to stand in front of the house, sir. I was mad as hell, I can tell you. And the thing is that I love the idea of outsiders coming here, but the ones that came and stayed knew nothing about the countryside or the forest, and if they lost a child, there's no way it will be where the dead hares are 'cause I might know some things, but that doesn't include where lost children go. And here in town, we know nothing about those outsiders, sir, except that when they come here it's 'cause they're not loved anymore, not wanted somewhere else. That's all I know, anyway. And in the countryside, hands are what we value, just hands. But what do those people bring? Some ridiculous idea of country life. And just to make matters worse, we have the end of the world looming over us. The world falling apart by the minute. I can tell you, I was mad as hell, sir.

The house was empty; had been that way for three years. We all knew that lovers from Pueblo Grande went there to have sex. Esteban said he could hear them moaning. And that's fine by me 'cause, when there's nowhere else to go, town property is for that too. And lovers have uncontrollable passions, so there's nothing for it. And that's why if the house were mine, it would be half hotel and half walk-in clinic by now.

When I got home that day, I found Javier about to leave me produce from his plot on the doormat; it's a small plot of land, but he shares what he grows with us, just like Marco shares his weed and I share any leftover sobao sponge cakes from the grocery store. The house where I live is dark, all the windows face the forest, but we have a yard where we keep hens, rabbits, and a nanny goat Javier found at his door one day and declared that no, no, no way did he want a goat. Javier lives alone in the smallest house in town. His father died young and his mother went off and abandoned him. She hasn't come back. Here in town, we count her among the disappeareds 'cause some people say they saw her entering the forest in the early hours and she didn't come out again. But I don't talk about that to Javier. Nowadays he has a small house with a small plot of land, and a bar in Pueblo Grande – if we'd met in other circumstances, I'd have taken you there – Javier lets us smoke Marco's weed in the bar, and that's what we do some evenings.

'A family from the centre is coming to live here,' I told Javier. 'Here where?' he asked. 'Here in Jimena's house.' 'They're robbing the lovers of a bed,' he said. And I laughed, the way you did at what I said about the end of the world 'cause I was imagining the couples with their bodies all fired up with desire. Later, I said to my mother, 'Jimena's house has been sold, Ma.' And she said, 'What's that to me?' I didn't laugh that time 'cause I was imagining all the secrets the house held and saying to myself that poor Jimena had been all alone in that big house, living her life there for so many years, filling it with nothing, all alone with her unhappiness, her dislikes, her radio; even her cat abandoned her. And I was frightened, the way children are and the way some people fear the end of the world, 'cause if hatred is inherited in small towns, loneliness is too, and my gut started burning again and I felt such deep sorrow that I thought it was exactly like the end of the world.

'Why are they coming here, Ma?' I asked. 'For their own reasons, child. We need new blood.' 'And anyway,' added my father, who was in the yard with the rabbits, 'if what they say about things coming to an end is true, it's makes no difference if they come. We'll all end up going.' With all my heart I wanted to yell at them – and I never yell; I might raise my voice, sir, but I never shout. And I shouted that they must be plain dumb if they believed the world was going to end and it was okay to welcome outsiders. Didn't they remember, I asked, didn't they remember the Dolores family? They turned up years ago and we welcomed them with open arms, then they managed to buy up half the land around here, and now they exploit our labour. I'll have more to say about the Dolores family later, sir.

There's no way you can know it, but folks here play games with their memories, they prefer to be surprised a thousand times by the same things rather than remember them. 'People come here to stay 'cause they're not loved, not wanted somewhere else,' I finally told my parents. 'Now, see what you've done. Your sister's soiled herself,' my father said. My sister's empty-headed and can't even shit on her own. That was the first day I thought of leaving, sir. I suppose it was the first day I took note of the end of the world too.

I said that to Nora in the evening, while I was removing the food she didn't swallow from her mouth – I'm the one who feeds Nora 'cause my parents are weary of her – and in that sisterly space I told her, 'Nora, I think the world as I've known it so far is getting narrower; life here is a small pond, Nora, like in the song, life here has no worth.' What I didn't tell my sister was that the world as I'd known it up to then felt too narrow; I was afraid of being left alone, like Jimena, in a house that was too big in a town that was too small.

I have the feeling that the man enjoys listening to me. I've often been told I have a pleasant voice and I get passionate when I speak, which makes people want to listen. The man is comfortable with me. It doesn't matter if you're not interested in what I'm telling you, I say, you're an accomplice now, you're abetting me in my escape. You don't leave this world's end, you escape from it. And, anyway, you have no choice, you have to listen to me 'cause I asked you that favour and you accepted. And the man smiles at me in a kind way. People sometimes look at me like you just did, I tell him. People from Pueblo Grande, people who aren't from here, look at me like you just did. And the man blushes and looks into the forest. And I look into the forest too.

Jimena's house was transformed in less than three weeks. Less than three weeks, sir. Word was that the family from Madrid had money and everyone was wondering how much they'd paid to have the largest house in town renovated in such a short time. 'They really are in a hurry to move here, Catalina,' I said one day at noon as we stood with our arms folded watching the front door being changed. 'You really are taking a dislike to this place,' she replied with a hint of scorn, 'cause she doesn't find these four streets as suffocating as I do. They'd painted the window frames, doors and walls white and I thought they were a pair of ignorant city people who might know about other things but had no idea how lovely unpainted stonework is. You don't believe me? Unpainted stonework is lovely, and it's not just me saying so; it's clear as daylight. Stone tells stories. The unease I felt about that family of outsiders, a family I still hadn't met, rose from my stomach to my throat, growing and growing, the way my nails do, or my hair, or the burning in my gut.

For the three weeks the work took, everybody in town spent their days gathered around the house. Juana even moved her and her brother's chairs there. And it seemed like they'd stopped worrying about the end of the world. They sat and watched and noted what they saw, they commented or didn't comment, they applauded a job well done and brought water and cold cuts for the workmen. Catalina used to hang around there in the mornings too, as though her hands couldn't be busy else-where. Then, in the evenings, in the bar, she'd detail the progress to Marco, Javier and me. And they'd tell me that if I was going to be so distrustful of the outsiders, I'd end up hating them, and in small towns hatred is more dan-gerous than guns, the forest, or illness. No, no, no way, I'd say. It's not hatred, just curiosity, I'm curious about why. I'm wondering who's stopped loving them, stopped wanting them around, so they've had to leave.

One evening in the bar, Catalina said the house was ready, and then she burst into tears. I was getting less and less tolerant of Catalina's tears 'cause while my sister only ever cries when her body pains her, Catalina cries for everything my sister doesn't, and then some. You won't be aware of it, sir, but the same used to happen at school when we were little. She'd cry when the dirt track left white dust on her shoes. Or when she got splinters in her fingers in the playground. And the tears would go on and on, so if the splinter happened in the morning, she'd be still crying at sundown. I'd pinch her cheek to get her attention and say that if she went on crying for every inch the world moved in its orbit, she'd end up dying at home from dehydration. And now we don't go to school anymore, she still cries over things like the work being finished on Jimena's house or the stupid end of the world. To be honest, I've always thought the reason Catalina spends her whole life crying is the suspicion she feels about anything that takes her from her own front door. And that burn on her leg, of course; she'll spend her whole life crying over that.

'And why are you so sorry that they've finished work on the house?' asked Marco with that aggressive look he always wears when he doesn't know something. 'Well, what am I going to do in the mornings now?' 'Go back to the chickens,' I answered. Catalina works in a chicken hatchery in Pueblo Grande. The two of us left school at the same time; when we reached seventeen, we said not one year more and dropped out. School wasn't for us. I knew that life was waiting outside, and that my head is my greatest asset, but inside those four walls I felt like an animal in a zoo, an animal in a tiny cage. And Catalina wanted money for the operation on her injured leg. I started work in my parents' store and Catalina earns a living at the hatchery. 'And what's worse,' she said, wiping the liquid from her cheeks, 'It's spring.' Marco glanced at me and we both laughed, and Javier, who was serving another table, laughed too. Nobody had mentioned the end of the world again 'cause it had us cracking up, but Catalina was always crying about it, and we weren't about to start mopping up and painting over leaks on the floor of the house. In fact, by the beginning of April, no one at all was talking about the end of the world, even though we had a daily minute's silence and ribbons still hung in the windows. 'Don't be silly, Catalina,' said Marco. 'It's true, true, true,' she said, 'This is no laughing matter, they're still talking about it in the newspapers. I've searched it on the internet, and this is going to be our last summer, everything's going to end, the countdown has started, and I don't want to die.' And then a married couple from Pueblo Grande who'd been listening to us came up and the man said, 'There's none so deaf as those who will not hear,' and I was thinking to myself that it was just as well I left school, that education doesn't free you from stupidity, when the man added, 'Take the mayor, for example. He knows a thing or two and he believes in the end of the world.' His wife looked down at her feet. And I can tell you, sir, looking at that woman, I saw what the future held for me in a town like this. For the first time – and I mean this – for the very first time I saw the days and the weeks becoming years if my life were reduced to this: if I stay here, sir, what awaits me is a life subjected to ridiculous beliefs, to the dullness of a long marriage. And, accompanying the couple to the door of the bar, I said, 'All's well that ends well.' As I watched them walk away, with my pupils dilated from the marijuana, my gut began to burn again and my fears grew like a tree in its native soil. Can't they see that we carry the end of the world inside ourselves? That the world's end is this place, this forest, and this vast oblivion we live in? But I didn't say that out loud.

When I returned to the table, I sat beside Catalina, with the fire rising up my throat, and from the bottom of my heart said, 'Why don't you go cry outside? You can wash the streets with your tears.' And even Marco – though he was always the rudest of the four of us – couldn't hide his surprise, and Catalina suddenly stopped being sad and the tear that was about to fall stayed put. I had the urge to add that I hoped her eyes dried up, but I didn't. I'm rarely cruel. You truly have to believe me, cruelty isn't my thing, but there's something I've inherited from this land that, just sometimes, makes me that way. Because in small places, people grow evil, are capable of anything, capable of skinning rabbits and letting themselves get accustomed to the sight of cruelty, and that sticks like a dose of flu, 'cause it has to do with weariness, with forgetting, with the four streets we live in. At that moment, I wanted to be cruel to Catalina, I couldn't bear her tears, particularly when they were for something I considered as absurd as the end of the world. And it could have been worse, I could have said, 'Klutzy, get out of this bar and go cry in the forest, you might get lost there.' Or, 'Not even those chickens you raise love you.' Because very few people have loved Catalina and she knows nothing about that, about true love. Or I could have said her leg reminded me of a cow's wrinkly arsehole, but I didn't 'cause then we'd have had to spend the whole night baling out the tears from her eyes. But I was a little cruel and it felt wonderful. 'If you believe in the end of the world, don't come around my house celebrating that you're still alive, 'cause I won't open the door, Klutzy.' Blame it on my dilated pupils. Javier left the counter and came across to say, 'Ignore her, Catalina,' and then he grabbed my arm and said, 'What's eating you?'

The man looks at me and this time his expression is serious. Don't look at me that way, don't look at me, I tell him, and I continue my story.

The thing is that when I was born, Ma had been mother to Nora for three years. The only difference between three-year-old Nora and Nora now is that she's lost her milk teeth. When I was born my mother knew about other things, but not about babies as wide awake as fawns. With Nora and her damaged brain, my mother learned that life can be cruel and that prevented her happiness from developing. Javier and Nora were born on the same day of the same year and the neighbours took turns visiting one baby then the other. In a town where babies are scarce, you'll understand that two turning up at once is a major event, as big as the August Festival. They say all that coming and going from one house to the next was like a trip from the coast to the forest, and entering my home and seeing my parents holding tight to Nora, with her empty eyes, was just like thinking about the forest, as though they could see the depths of woodlands in her little face. And they say that the sight of Javier was like seeing a strong calf, full of life, latching to its mother nipple as if he knew hunger before he was born; he was like the sea in the sunlight on a gusty day. Javier's joyful home was different from mine when Big Lea and my dad became parents, and as that difference weighed on Javier's mother, she used to bring her son along to help my parents with Nora, and in exchange my mother left fruit from the store on her doormat. I guess Javier's mum was counting her lucky stars for getting the healthy baby. She felt sorry for my family. That happens a lot with

Nora, we feel sorry, feel pity. But I always say pity is for sad people, and here, in our home, there's always been happiness; we cry very little here, it isn't something we know much about so we don't know how to cry properly. And anyway, sir, pity's like the plague. It's contagious.

And then when I was born, three years after Nora, the first people to come to see me were Javier and his mum. My mother always says that the instant Javier saw my bright eyes he came in close and sniffed me. Like I said, I've never been able to smell. Although with time, I've learned to do it in a different way and now, if there's one thing I know, it's that my mother smells like limes piled up in a basket and my father smells of mornings in the orchard when everything's ready to be picked. I've always imagined Javier's smell to be like one of those oranges you can open without a knife and the juice dribbles onto your hand. I'd have liked to have smelled Javier when he grabbed my arm to ask what was eating me. Or for him to have smelled me.

What was I going to answer, sir? Even I hardly knew what was eating me! So I answered that it was nothing, that I was thinking about wanting to leave town; or at least that's what I should have told him, and if I had everything would be simpler now, but I what I actually said was that I had a fire in my gut. And between clenched teeth, he said, 'You've been acting weird since Jimena's house was sold.'

And, to be honest, I had no idea how to explain my moodiness, how to say that deep down, deep, deep down inside me, I was afraid of the end of the world 'cause we were already living in the world's end, and if dying was going to mean living forever in this town, I didn't want to die.

After all the tensions of that evening, when they dropped me off at home, I stood in the doorway smoking the last of the weed. The countryside is never silent and nighttime in this town is full of noises. Even at that hour, someone was tending cows. I imagined telling the newcomers not to touch my native soil 'cause if I ever managed to get away, I'd leave my heart buried here. And while I was imagining that, the forest was watching me. 'You already have everything, what more do you want?' I asked it. And as though the darkness was an open window, the wind blew straight in my face and I can tell you it was warm for April. That wind stoked the fire in my gut, making it burn even stronger. And do you know what? I'm sure that if the people who disappeared decided to return from the forest, they'd come to me and say, 'Don't worry, Lea, it won't hurt.' Because those words always precede pain or sorrow. Like when a doctor says them and then you never forget the pain. Or like the end of the world that, if it could talk, would say to us, 'Don't worry, it won't hurt.' But it will. And if anyone ever returns from that forest, they'll bring pain with them. The marijuana I was smoking that night brought childhood memories of my sister and I stopped seeing the forest before me and instead saw myself as a little girl and my mother treating an infection in the teeth of a Nora whose body was hanging all loose. Taking my sister in your arms is like picking up a dead calf. Nora was letting the pinkish dribble run down her chin while looking hard at me; my sister's always looking at me; my sister's never going to stop looking at me.

When I need to stop talking for a second a silence falls between the man and me. He's good at silence. I like you, I say, and continue.

And then Marco came up and grabbed my arm hard and he too said: 'What's eating you?' I brushed his hand away 'cause I didn't want Marco touching my body. Marco really doesn't know his own strength and I didn't want him touching me. 'So, what's eating you?' he asked again. And we came to sit here, on the edge of the woodlands, just like we are now. 'Your problem is you don't cry enough,' he said and continued, 'Yes, yes, it's true; people who don't cry tears cry anger instead.' And I had to laugh 'cause he's the one always getting angry, the one with a bad temper, the one who sometimes frightens me, the one who's – sometimes – mean to us, to animals, and even treats his own land badly, and when he gets really drunk, then goes home and pisses all around the bed where his parents are sleeping.

The man laughs. Yes, yes, he does, and his mother says, 'Fifteen hours in labour and look what I got for it.' And the man laughs and I laugh with him.

Marco acts that way 'cause he doesn't want to be here either, but he doesn't know anything about anything. And there's not a thing he does know that would be useful anywhere else. He only knows how to work the land 'cause his father took him out of school when he was thirteen. Don't look at me that way, I know it isn't allowed, but we're so remote here, nobody found out. This is the world's end, the last point on the map. Nobody comes here to check if the children are in school or not. And now all Marco knows is how to till the land, take in other people's harvests, and tend their cows. And then he tells me I don't cry enough. I felt like asking, 'What do you know?' And I did. And I added that tears are always for other people to see. And Catalina goes around sharing what's inside her through her tears and I don't understand that. Sorrow can't be cried. You keep sorrow inside and it heals. Pain and sorrow don't need to be cried over, if they stay there inside, they disappear, the way a river disappears when there's no water, and then all that's left is a deep dirt track that reminds you that sorrow was once there. And Marco repeated that my problem was that I didn't cry enough. And I replied, 'No, no, that isn't true. My pain and sorrow heal differently.' And rage, the weed, and the dark flared up like the fire in my gut. 'You'll never leave here, Lea. This land won't let us go,' he told me.

Marco has always been fond of me. While Javier and Nora were born on the same day of the same year, Marco and I came into the world in the same year, but five days apart. I looked like a freshly landed salmon and he was like one of those dead hares the lost dogs eat. The ones your dog's eating right now. The thing is that I was born bursting with life and Marco very nearly didn't make it to his third day. Marco has always been fond of me. When we were kids, I wanted to be around Javier, but Marco was small and frail, always feeling tired, and I'd take his arm, tug it, and sometimes pull him along to keep up with me. And nowadays, when he looks at me, he thanks me for having pulled him along when he was so weak he could hardly walk. But when his body changed and his father set him to working the land, Marco went from being a calf to a fighting bull, a raging bull with blood on his back. He's always been fond of me, but he knows nothing about love.

'Come on, come on,' Marco said. 'Follow me.' And though, as you'll understand, I was suspicious, I followed him. Walking with his head bowed, Marco reminded me of the dead hare he was when he was small. There's no silence in the night here, you know. You can tell there are ghosts, bodies that have been trapped here in town, as will happen to Marco; when he dies, he'll be left wandering these streets 'cause he'll never know anything else. Not me, I'll be walking dead in some other place. 'Here,' he said and held out a black marker pen, one of those thick ones they use to write on the cattle. And I looked at what stood before me and it was the whitewashed stone of Jimena's house. Nobody was living there yet, so it was all closed up. Marco winked at me and silent laughter welled up, and then I laughed aloud so hard it infected Marco and would have infected you too if you'd been there. I uncapped the marker and wrote on the whitewashed housefront.

IF YOU SMELL ANYTHING, BARK

The day the outsiders arrived, it was my turn to look after Nora. That's what I used to do when my father was working for the Dolores family. I didn't like him working for them 'cause he never knew how to say things straight and the Doloreses didn't treat him well. I was always telling him that we all get what's coming to us, and I'm saying that 'cause I know that someday life is going to explode in the face of that family and, sooner or later, something bad will happen to them. 'Dad, the pay is awful. You shouldn't work more than half an hour for the money you earn,' I'd tell him. But Dad didn't like stirring the pot and he'd reply, 'No, my girl. I do it so that someday they'll give me the pear trees and so on, little by little, until I manage to make a deal with them for a piece of land.' My father knew about apples, about orchards, about animals, but he knew very little about talking and nothing at all about deals.

Marco works for them too; my father takes care of the fruit and he cares for the livestock. But Marco gets a lot of money out of the Dolores family 'cause he's never still. And nothing hurts him. If he has to tend the cattle at three in the morning, he just does it; and if a cow gets stuck in the mud, he doesn't need help pulling it out. I don't know what he spends the money on. He sometimes gave my father a little 'cause he's always been fond of me. And though he'll never know anything about love, he does understand basic needs. When I found out that Marco was giving my father money, I started leaving sobaos from the store at his door; he likes them and I have no other way of saying thanks. But I was saddened for my father, just as I'm sometimes saddened that my mother can't bear the burden of my sister. Anyway, so when he went to work in the Dolores family's orchard, I'd stay with Nora, and that way my mother got a bit of a break too. Because she doesn't know I know, but when she's alone in the store, she sings.

When Nora shits, she makes a rumbling sound. And since I can't smell, that's how I know she needs changing. It's sometimes hard to lie her down 'cause Nora's hands are always on the move, like she's trying to remind me that she has no memory or understanding, and even though she's never quiet for an instant, she still doesn't understand. If I lie her down to change her, she doesn't understand. If I sit her at the table to eat, she doesn't understand. My sister doesn't understand life and she never will. But I believe that with me by her side, she understands a little more 'cause I can still bear the burden she is and I still hold her gaze. My parents, on the other hand, are tired and they know nothing about gazes, and Nora watches them from sunrise to sunset 'cause that's all Nora does: look, shit, and swallow when you put food in her mouth. My parents are so tired, they don't know what to do with themselves. When I lie her down, I stroke her face and give her my hands so she can see that I don't always understand life either, and then my sister is calmer and her legs aren't so heavy. She has a real bushy area between her legs, like the woodlands, and I tell her she's lovely when she's had a shit. I like to believe she laughs to herself. When she was small, she used to put earth in her mouth. My parents would take her out to the plot behind the house and Nora would grab handfuls of earth and put them in her mouth. And my mother would rush to stop her, but Nora always ended up with black teeth. I used to take the worms and twigs out so she could eat the earth safely. When my mother saw me doing that, she'd exclaim, 'What a pair of laurels I've been given.' I never understood what she meant. Do you? Bad luck, I suppose. See what bad luck I have to bear. Something like that maybe. She didn't understand that we couldn't deny Nora something she'd chosen. The thing is that Nora doesn't make choices, she accepts. She doesn't eat earth these days 'cause nobody takes her out to the plot, which is a pity.

When I was changing my sister's nappy this morning, our neighbour's dog – it often sneaks into the house in the mornings and makes itself at home – started to bark. What do you want, dog? What do you want? And it wagged its tail. What do you want, dog? What do you want? And a car passed the front door of the house. I left Nora in bed with the nappy half-changed and her ass unwashed. You see, in this town we only close the door when it rains or when we go to bed. And so the door was wide open. 'Quiet, dog,' I said, with the sun shining straight in my eyes, like it was in yours before you came to sit in the shade with me. My father says I have backcountry eyes. 'Here comes Little Lea with her little backcountry eyes.' He means I sometimes look suspiciously at things from having always lived in a small town and having been born near a dangerous forest. Or 'cause I'm scared of things I don't know. Whatever, it was those eyes that watched a car pass by slowly. And inside the car were a sleeping woman and a baby in the back seat. The man driving was wearing sunglasses and he seemed to be complaining about the state of the road, and I imagined him saying, 'These huge potholes will ruin the car.' But the woman was asleep and her mussed-up hair was pressed against the window. 'They're here, Nora,' I said, 'They're here.' And as my eyes were fixed on the car and the dog went on barking, I didn't notice Catalina arriving.

'Lea, you deaf or something? I've been calling you from the corner. It's the newcomers! You should see the crowd in the square. And I think your mother's preparing a welcome basket for them.' Catalina doesn't have backcountry eyes; she has a child's eyes, the eyes of a fish that's strayed from the school. The eyes of somebody who doesn't know. I imagined Catalina running behind the car, shouting my name so I'd look out of the window to watch the arrival of the newcomers and that gave me a warm feeling, like in that song that goes, 'I'm a breeze without air, nothing to anybody.' I felt bad about being rude to her the day before. 'We have to see what they do when they get to the house,' she said, 'someone has written "unloved and unwelcome" on the front.'

And the man looks at me and I look into the forest.

Catalina was born, and she was the only one that year. It was a very sad year, you see, 'cause her mother died almost as soon as she popped out. The mayor declared a week's mourning before the funeral. But we don't even reach two hundred inhabitants so one evening was more than sufficient for everyone to attend the vigil and Catalina's mother was beginning to smell. By the end of the week, the town stank worse than a stagnant pond. Her father quickly stopped loving Catalina and neglected her. The neighbours say she used to cry so much at night you could hear her all around town. And she goes on and on crying. 'She's crying for her mother,' some said. And others replied, 'No, no, that isn't it, she's crying because her father doesn't take her out of her cot.' Whatever the case, Catalina has never had much love and now she loves too much. And she forgives people too easily, but that's so they won't stop loving her. Catalina is attracted to Marco, but Marco is never going to know how to love her: she's too much of a woman for him.

'Who wrote that on the house?' I asked Catalina. 'Well, Esteban says he saw two people last night, I think they must have come from Pueblo Grande.' And my eyes stopped being backcountry and I said she was most likely right; if I told her it had been Marco and me, she'd start crying and ask what we had against the newcomers. That's what she'd say, sir. 'You go,' I replied, 'I'm busy.' And I went on changing Nora, who was rumbling a little louder than usual. Catalina has always been slightly scared of Nora, so she limped off toward the square as if she were running.

'Did you see, Nora? Did you see them?' I asked. 'They'll go crazy living here in town. You'll see, when they realise how slowly time passes. You'll see. A leopard doesn't change its spots; they'll flip out, start heading for the forest, Nora. Because a leopard has spots and, here, outsiders head for the forest. But I've already learned not to get attached to anyone from outside, and especially not to love any of the ones that come here. And those people today are here to stay. Just like the Doloreses years ago, before you and I existed, Nora. The same thing happened then; everybody welcoming them with open arms, and look at that family now, exploiting the very people who made a space for them. But no one else seems to see it that way. Some idiot goes around saying that the world is ending, and everyone here believes him and is frightened, and they're mourning day in and day out. And when people from the city turn up at this point on the map nobody's interested in, we don't say a word. We applaud them. It's 'cause folk here are bored with so much green and so much bad weather; they don't ask questions. But Nora, who in their right mind would want to come to this town?'

The arsonist that must have taken up residence in my gut lit another match and the burning flared up again. I told all that to my sister, but I'd also seen something in the way that woman was sleeping in the car. Something I couldn't put my finger on at that moment. Like the woman looking down at her feet in the bar, the woman who'd made me glimpse my future in this town. But the outsider sleeping in the car seemed to give me a glimpse of something more; something dark that I didn't recognise. That's all I know. And it made me really mad 'cause when I don't know something, the first thing I do is get mad. And the small, controlled flame in my gut was suddenly the kind of fire that leaves destruction in its wake. And I knew, just knew what was going to happen. I knew that the moment they set foot here, my curiosity would rear its head. You never learn, Lea, I told myself. Here in town, it's a bad idea to be curious when something new appears; curiosity is for new things in other places. And the reason is that it hurts when those newcomers leave or get lost.

And then I started to ruminate, like cows do, sir; just as now I'm ruminating on everything I've been telling you. 'Nora,' I said, taking her hands and looking into her eyes. She looked back, which she rarely does 'cause Nora doesn't really know how to look back. 'You know me,' I went on, 'You know I try. I try to be more distant, try not to get attached. You know I've got the whole backcountry in my eyes. And I'm wondering, Nora, wondering why people who can choose where they go come here, only to leave in no time at all, to get tired of it in the blink of an eye. And once more I'll be left thinking that people only come here to leave again, while those of us from here aren't going anywhere.' I said all that to my sister. And then I added, 'A leopard has spots, outsiders head for the forest, and I choose curiosity and the heart.' And Nora didn't make her rumbling noise or move her hands. It was like she understood. I was deep in thought when I suddenly realised that instead of anger, my gut was burning with anticipation. 'Nora, how about if I do it? Go there and say no, no, don't pay attention to that message. I mean it, you're welcome in the world's end. Say my name is Lea and if you need anything, you'll find me in one of the houses down the hill. And I'll try to be firm and tell myself that nothing interesting can happen in these four streets, anything new this land accepts is always the mirage of a life we don't have, but I'm bursting with curiosity and good deeds. I don't want to be friendly to them, the countryside and small towns aren't friendly, but my gut is burning with the desire to understand or to question; I don't know, just don't know. Whatever, I have to see them so I can be comfortably mad about their presence. And I'm telling you all this, Nora, so you'll listen and take it in. You have to make an effort to get things straight in your head and your body for a moment. Yes, yes, you know that's true. Listen, Nora, I'll be gone for twenty minutes, maybe less. But you need to stay here quietly. I'll be back in no time. And when I come back, I promise to brush your hair and braid it, and I'll take you outside to the plot like when we were kids, and I promise I'll give you earth to eat. Just don't move, Nora.' And I looked at the neighbour's dog and said, 'Dog, stay there with her and if she moves, bark. If you smell something, bark. Bark loud if she falls or if she shits.' It knows about things like that. And I went along the street Catalina had hobbled up, leaving Nora there with the dog and the front door wide open.

I sprinted and caught up with Catalina just past the grocery store. Because of her limp, I can always catch her, even when she's running. On the way, I saw my mother in the store; she was singing as she prepared her basket. She'd added fresh vegetables that had just arrived from Pueblo Grande and apples from the Doloreses' orchard my father had picked from the trees the week before. I grabbed Catalina's arm and we stood there between Juana and Marga from the pharmacy in Pueblo Grande.

The car arrived and we all watched it, squinting our eyes to see in the strong sunlight. Like I said, sir, it was hot as hell for April. 'Marco says they've spent all their savings on the house,' said Catalina, and I replied, 'Don't believe everything Marco tells you.' But the thing is that Marco always finds out about everything. It's 'cause he gets around; he spends whole days in the bars in Pueblo Grande and sometimes even weeks in the city by the sea. But we don't know exactly what he does there. 'Don't listen to Marco. He's a bullshitter.' 'Don't be so distrustful, Lea,' said Catalina.

The blonde woman who'd been sleeping in the car was awake now and looking out the side window at us all. The boy – he was four or five years old – had his mouth open and seemed to be crying. Bawling his head off. I dropped Catalina's arm and she asked where I was going, said I should stay with her. But I went on ahead with a hand to my eyes so I could open them wider. I stopped near Esteban and he touched his rifle 'cause he wasn't expecting to find me so close and Esteban is scared of me. The first person to get out of the car was the man and I went up to say hello. He said hello back and then spotted the graffiti. I silently watched the woman getting out of the car and said hello to her too. 'The whole town's here to look at you,' I added. 'Pay no mind to that writing,' said Esteban, 'Here, the mules are human, and as they're not given to thinking, they do things like that.'

The blonde woman tittered. Her laughter was different to ours; it was the sort of restrained, well-bred laughter we rarely hear in this town, and as breeding means something else here, it felt out of place. 'Laugh away, open your mouth if you want,' I said, 'In these parts, we show our teeth when we laugh.' And the man took the crying child in his arms. 'Thanks very much for the welcome,' he said to me. And before they went indoors,

I told them that my name was Little Lea, that Big Lea was my mother and the owner of the general store, and she'd be coming by soon to give them a basket. Then all the other bystanders began to chant their names: I'm Marga from the pharmacy in Pueblo Grande; I'm Julito's sister Juana, but now I'm just Juana; I'm Marcela and that's Adolfo, we own the Tudanca cattle grazing upriver. And Catalina went up and said, I'm Catalina and I raise chickens at the Jorge brothers' hatchery, and her chubby cheeks went as hard as hazelnuts and red as the sun at seven in the evening. Then Esteban said, I'm Esteban, and that's all he had to say 'cause Esteban could only say I'm Esteban, the most fearful man in the world – which is how he's known in town – or he could have said, I'm Esteban, the man who killed Lea's dog, but he just said his name. And I'm Father Antón from the church; I say mass here on Sundays and ring the bells. I didn't look at Antón 'cause – I haven't mentioned this yet – I don't want to know anything about God. Sometimes, when Antón catches sight of me in town, he calls out, 'Where's Little Lea who rarely sets foot in my church off to?' And he sells me puzzle books for teens. And I often reply, 'Antón,' – 'cause I refuse to call him Father; I've already got a father and Antón is only a father of sheep – 'if you haven't got anything good to say, say nothing, and I'm less pretty when I'm quiet but a closed mouth suits you fine.'

And the man laughs again.

After that, the newcomers took all their bags from the car and carried them indoors without even introducing themselves. The neighbours sat nearby to watch them open the windows to air thfe house. Catalina stayed there too, sitting with the old folk. I turned on my heels and went straight home, with my gut burning and repeating two phrases: a) Who's stopped loving you? and b) I need to get out of this town.

AS I WAS LOST THERE ALSO, THE TWO OF US DID MEET

Javier is a man of very few words. He communicates in other ways; for example, if he has to tell me how he's feeling, he does it with his thoughts first. I'm attracted to Javier, but he's afraid of me 'cause if he's a strawberry tree that's almost a bush, I'm a sequoia. I'm the tallest conifer in existence, one whose trunk never breaks and gives off a scent, and though I might not know anything about scents, I imagine mine to be like a sequoia with a thick trunk and smooth bark. Well, I'm that tree and I believe that I've always been too big for Javier, even though I know that he's fond of me and we've kissed, he doesn't have the courage to love and desire me the way I'd like to love and desire him.

You see, sir, nobody's loved and desired me that way yet. I mean the way couples do. I'd like to learn about that with Javier 'cause I like him; I've liked him since he sniffed me when I was a newborn baby. And the strange thing is that we have this inner bond; we have the same gestures and ways of being that regular couples have, but when I say, 'Javier, I really, really like you,' he doesn't say a word. The point is that Javier is a man who communicates in other ways. Like wolves, sir. Do you know about wolves? When they're going to kill, first they say what they're thinking and then they kill. They say it by showing their teeth. And after they've done that, they kill. Or they leave a mark on you. Javier's like a wolf; first he shows me his teeth, then he finds a soft spot and leaves his mark on me. Javier only talks when the wound is already stinging. One day he looked at me differently and I knew he had something to say. 'What is it, Javier?' I kept asking; when he doesn't speak, I insist. And he ran his tongue over his teeth. Then he looked into my doe eyes and that's where he left his mark, saying that he'd been seeing his father at night. His dead father, sir. The father he never loved much 'cause his father wasn't really his father. I don't know if you believe in such things. In small places we do; but that's 'cause we have to find reasons for so many noises, and in town they say the ones who disappear into the forest are watching us while we sleep.

The man looks at me as though he understands small places perfectly.

'Tell me another, Javier,' I said, and that laugh burst from my throat and echoed as far as the houses in the lower part of town, the ones that get flooded when the river overflows. 'Yes, yes, I'm not kidding. I see the man who was my father, but I don't speak to him 'cause I'm scared he'll never go away,' Javier answered. Sometime after he'd told me that, a nanny goat appeared in his house and Javier is convinced it's his father come to see him. The father he didn't love. The father – who wasn't his father – had come back to the world's end that way 'cause he thought maybe his son – who wasn't his son – would love him better as a nanny goat. And the goat – it was already old when it arrived – lives in the yard of our house now, next to the hens 'cause Javier said his house was too small and the nanny goat's no trouble at all. I sometimes stroke it, but if you touch a goat too often, the smell sticks. Did you know that? A while later, I asked Javier if he was still seeing his father and he said he wasn't.

I'm telling you this 'cause, even if you don't believe in ghosts or dead people who hang around a place, I want you to lie to me; I've never asked anyone to do that before. But I'd like you to lie and say that people do hang around after they've died. When I've told you what I'm going to tell you next, I want you to tell me that lie. Can you do that?

The man looks at me with a mix of tenderness and something strange I can't quite get a hold on. I look back at him, knowing that I'm most likely asking too much.

Like I was saying, while I was walking along the cobbled street to my house, ruminating about wanting to leave town, the clock struck twelve noon and the bells rang to signal the minute's silence for the end of the world. The hubbub of the townsfolk chatting near Jimena's house died down and my shoes on the cobbles were the only sound in the square. And when there were just a few seconds to go before they all started up again, the neighbour's dog began to bark and, as it raced toward me, you could hear its paws too. I frowned and thought Nora must have shit herself again. But the dog met me halfway home and barked so loud, so very loud, sir, that it hurt my ears. 'Quiet, dog, quiet. I'm coming.' But I'm pretty smart and my intuition is like a dart to the centre of the target, so I started to run home, and those yards seemed like miles.

Then suddenly, sir, Marco's arms were around me, bringing me to a halt. And he held me so tight I couldn't breathe and said, 'Don't go there, Lea.' 'What are you talking about, Marco? Let go of me.' 'Don't go there, Lea.' 'Marco, I can't breathe. Let go of me.' And I began to wriggle, and with Marco's body blocking my way, I felt like I was set in reinforced concrete. 'He's dead, he's dead.' But Marco didn't let go and held my head like a vice. Then I said I hated him, said he was suffocating me, told him to let me go. And Marco said no, no. And the neighbour's dog kept barking. And if anybody attacks me, I'm like a brown bear, so I sank my teeth into Marco's arm so deeply that when he let go and I saw my father lying dead outside his own home with a wound in his head, I had a slight taste of blood in my mouth.

Sir, I know all anyone needs to know about death. I know all anyone needs to know about mourning. Death, sir, death is just a few days of tears. But I can't deny that it's essentially an end of the world, a brief explosion that upsets everything and gives rise to a tremendous desire to flee from where you are.

Javier's story is that my scream was audible as far as Pueblo Grande and Catalina says that when she heard my shriek, the scar on her leg started to hurt as though it had never healed. I don't know about that. I guess I know about other things. But anyway, that screaming made my mother drop the basket just as she was approaching the outsiders' front door and the apples went rolling across the square, the chocolates stuck to the ground and the eggs . . . Oh, the eggs! All broken on the cobbles. And Catalina called to my mother, 'Wait for me, Big Lea! Wait for me!' And neither of them realised that the shock had caused Esteban to shoot himself in the left foot and a trail of blood was tingeing the fallen green apples a dark, deep red.

Don't look at me, sir. Don't look at me that way.

My father might not have known about other things, but, I can tell you, he certainly did know how to love. When I was small, he'd take me to the river and hold me so I didn't slip on the wet, mossy stones. He'd inspect my hands for cuts. Then he'd carry me home in his arms and if Marco, Catalina or Javier was with us, he'd carry them on his back. My father was a horse, but people treated him like a mule.

The sight of my father's dead body brought to mind the time he told me to choose one of the rabbits he kept in the yard. After I'd made my choice, he set it to one side and that rabbit lived apart from the others and I was allowed to play with it, stroke it, and give it a name. He killed the other rabbits one by one. First he'd feed them up and then later they'd feed his family. I always felt bad about choosing a rabbit 'cause I wanted to save all the ones that were skinned.

And the man's expression is serious as he looks at me, the kind of expression people put on when they notice grief in others.

Well, the fact is that when I saw my father lying there dead I remembered the lucky rabbits that died of old age, with their faces all sharp and narrow. And my dead father was just the same, but with his head smashed in 'cause he'd tumbled down a hillside in the Dolores farm when he was trying to catch a rabbit. Marco picked him up and carried him home on his back. Marco has always been a pack animal, not a horse. After my scream, the only sound was Nora's teeth chattering like castanets.

The man looks at me and I look at the man. Like I said, sir, I have a backstory. And the man looks into the forest.

My father's vigil was held at home that same evening and the Dolores family took care of all the arrangements and paperwork. Their kindness had an ulterior motive: they wanted to stop us speaking out about the labour conditions on their land. I wish I'd known about such things, but I know nothing about struggles and exploitation, and neither does my mother or Marco, much less any of those good-for-nothings crying for my father around the house. Because all the townsfolk gave up watching the newcomers and moved their chairs to surround my dead father. Catalina – who cried so hard that she soaked the kitchen floor – was saying that this, that this, this misfortune was just another proof of the end of the world and I – with few feelings and fewer words – ended by agreeing that the world was ending and she hugged me like you'd hug . . . I don't know who. Outside in the yard, I searched for my father's face among the live rabbits while I was thinking no, no, it can't be true that my father has died today but our lives will continue tomorrow. I was trying to convince myself, sir. And my father's face wasn't among the rabbits.

It's my belief, sir, that the end of the world is the perception that time – I mean the hands of the clock – no longer has the meaning we've been giving it up to now. And that's what I felt at my father's vigil. My father, who just a few hours before had been alive and working on the land he hoped to buy. I felt that the present, the past, and the future were there together in that house with people and rabbits all around the empty body of the man who had been my father just a few hours before. And I felt that my gut was burning 'cause time had ceased to have any meaning. The suspension of time is a signal that the world is killing itself, sir.

'Take your sister out of here. I can't bear it when she grinds her teeth,' my mother ordered. 'Ma, you look lovely in black,' I said. Her expression didn't change but she replied, 'My Little Lea, we're alone now.' And, sir, you can't imagine how my gut burned. And I felt like I was the rabbit she'd chosen to save. I asked Marco to put my sister in her wheelchair and wait for me outside. I squatted down to look the rabbits in the eyes one by one and then I opened their cage. 'What are you up to, Lea? You'll fill the house with rabbits,' said Catalina and I told her that those animals had almost more right to be mourning my father than so many boring neighbours.

My father was always reciting these lines to me, 'In a forest in China, the Chinese girl got lost, and as I was lost there also, the two of us did meet.' He'd say them when he put me to bed at night or when he was giving me my breakfast. Or sometimes he'd come to meet me from the school bus and greet me with that song. Then I grew up and my father taught me that when you plow the soil, when you're faced with the immensity of the country-side, you leave yourself open to death without giving it a second thought. Life is so marvellous, he'd say, the earth, the mountain, the forest or the countryside could gobble you up at any moment. And my father was killed by the earth he walked on, the countryside ate him the way he ate the rabbits. My father was a good man who always dreamed of recovering his land. The land he worked his whole life was his, it was his family's land, but he sold it to the Doloreses to buy a wheelchair for my sister. My father taught me that even though our life had its hardships, we didn't belong in that part of the world with a right to cry. And that's why I save my tears for my pillow. And I'll show you the sort of man my father was: one day he took my hand and said, 'If I die early, I'll gift you the years I haven't lived.' And now what, Dad? Now what? That's what I keep asking myself.

Marco, Catalina, and I were sitting on the bench across from the church rolling a joint when I looked at my sister in her chair and suddenly said, 'Nora, I think that if anyone had to leave us, it should have been you.' And Catalina said, 'Lea, you have a heart of stone.' Then Marco repeated, 'Your problem is you don't cry enough.' But I'm the sort who tells it like it is, and if Nora doesn't understand much about life, it's about time she had something to chew on. 'Nora,' I went on, 'Dad has left us, he isn't coming back, and when he told you this morning that he'd sing to you – my father used to sing, "As the boat was passing, the boatman said to me" to her – that was a lie. He isn't coming back.' Nora, who knew more than she let on, opened her mouth and I thought she was going to scream, but she just sat there looking at us with her jaw hanging loose. 'I'm sorry, Nora. Really sorry.' and then I dug my nails into her forearms, and though the neighbour's dog – it was there too – began to bark real loud, thinking I was attacking my sister, I went on digging my nails in 'cause Nora needed to cry, but she doesn't spill any tears over death or absence. And then the tears flowed almost of their own volition, the way they flowed on that Sunday in summer when Esteban killed the dog.

I'm quiet for a moment and the man takes advantage of my silence to say, 'Yes, those who leave us hang around.' I say thanks but tell him I don't need him to say that just yet. And the man looks at his feet and I continue my tale.

Javier is a man who walks tall and takes a long time doing things. I, on the other hand, go wherever I'm headed quickly. When I was small and the neighbours saw me around town, they'd call out, 'Here comes the flying gazelle! The flying gazelle!' That was 'cause I was always running. And when I was going to Catalina's house, I'd race along the paths 'cause you can enjoy the greenery better going fast. And more than once I came home with my legs scratched and my mother would fill the bathtub, wash me, and put peroxide on the cuts. And when it stung, I didn't say anything, 'cause Big Lea was always gentle and slow. You see, I'm the favourite of her two children, I'm the healthy one, the one with a future. So when my mother was cleaning my scratches, she did it as though I was a porcelain vase and she'd talk to me about the flowers she imagined growing in the forest we weren't allowed to enter. She'd tell me that Madonna lilies are as lazy as snails, which is why they don't grow fast, and that fuchsias are flowers that are always looking down, asking why their stems grow and carry them so far from the earth. I'd be spellbound, observing my mother's unhurried way of doing things and speaking. And it's that same pace, the same easy rhythm, I see in Javier when he's walking. Or when he's carving wood, 'cause he's been doing that since he was very young. His father – who isn't his father and is now a nanny goat – taught him to carve. And that's why he makes those delicate borders on tables and decorates pieces of furniture with endless spirals that take him days and days. Javier's house has the prettiest furniture in town; everyone says so. And whenever I sit and watch him carving the wood with more patience than I've ever possessed, I feel all emotional, sir, like when I hear the song that goes, 'my lonely soul, forever alone'.

In this town, sir, we only have deaths once in a blue moon so I don't know much about mourning or people who stop being here. When someone dies, Antón rings the bells at the wrong time so we all know that the person who was going to die has passed on. And then he posts an announcement on the corkboard in the church. There's nothing nice about our church. The one in Pueblo Grande is huge and beautiful and even if you don't believe in anything, it's a pleasure to be in there, an emotional experience, but what you feel when you see our small church, dark as the forest, is the desire to head in the opposite direction. When someone dies here, the usual people turn up, the usual people cry, and, if we're lucky, a relative comes from somewhere else. Marco has been our gravedigger since three years ago, when Jimena died, and he also takes charge of finding a space in the funeral plots, 'cause although very few people die here, sir, we've already got a whole history of others that are dead and buried. And Javier sees to the coffins. Another thing Marco's responsible for is the nameplace. I don't know who decided to call it that, but it's the most ridiculous thing I've ever heard, particularly as that's the one place where there aren't any names.

And I can tell you, sir, if you hadn't listened to me and had gone into the forest, you'd have ended up in the nameplace; it's the plot at the back of the graveyard dedicated to all those who've got lost in the woodlands. A wooden post is planted in the ground for each person who disappears, and now we have almost five hundred yards of them. Antón keeps the tally and whenever there's a burial he takes advantage to have posts planted for those who have disappeared since the last funeral. I remember that along with Jimena – before my father's death – ten poles were put up 'cause the year before a whole group of climbers from the city by the sea was lost. The nameplace is a way of reminding ourselves that there's an absence here, but in this small town we don't forget.

I was sorry it was Marco who buried my father, but no one could have done it better. Not that there was anyone else. What hurt me like a trap does a rat was that my father's coffin was buried unadorned. Javier refused to do it. That's right, sir; he said that carving a loved one pained his soul. 'No one's soul is more pained than mine,' I retorted. But Javier – I've already told you he doesn't say much – didn't open his mouth and my father went unadorned to the hole Marco had dug for him.

Our burials here are in the old style, sir. I don't know how they are where you live, but here the rituals aren't new. And that's even more true these days, with all this about the end of the world. Now, in 2012, we're still parading our dead through the streets with the family weeping behind. Then, during the wake, the first person to speak is Antón, followed by the mayor. But when we buried my father, the mayor wasn't present. I'm certain he didn't come 'cause he's afraid of me; he knows I speak my mind, even when the death is my father's. If he'd turned up, I'd have called him a liar to his face or said, 'A person herding lambs is just another sheep.' And he'd have gone so red he'd have had to put some money behind that walk-in clinic he promised us. But the mayor didn't come to my father's wake, and nor did his wife and six children.

I pushed Nora's wheelchair during the funeral procession. When we were passing Jimena's house, the outsider put his hand on my arm and I stopped dead 'cause the burning in my stomach and the desire to leave flared up again. My eyes went all backcountry, I mean really back, backcountry, sir. I didn't say anything, but he immediately asked what was going on, who'd died, and why we were parading him like that. 'It's my father. He took a tumble chasing a rabbit.' I replied. He looked surprised 'cause

68

dying from a tumble wasn't a death that his limited understanding could deal with. Or maybe he was thinking it
was a bad omen to be settling in with a funeral was going
on. I told him we were all going to the graveyard and that
we paraded our dead here in town. He offered lukewarm
condolences and before starting to push Nora's wheelchair again, I turned and said, 'In this town, things come
in pairs: when one child is born, another soon follows;
when someone gets lost in the forest, a dog without an
owner appears; when a cow behaves strangely, the end
of the world comes along, and when outsiders turn up,
my father dies.' And I went on pushing Nora's chair and
that burning – it was my grandmother Jimena filling my
stomach with flames; it was my dead father saying 'get out
of this town'; it was the end of the world – vanished like
the cold in summer.

We don't have a family plot or anything like that, so
Marco had dug a hole in the ground. Antón began to speak
and I didn't take my eyes off my mother, who had a veil
over her face. I watched her 'cause I'd never before seen
her suffering that kind of grief. Like I said, I know very,
very little about mourning sir. Will she ever sing again? I
thought. But I watched her carefully 'cause she reminded
me of the wooden statue of the Virgin in the church. And
that face has always scared me. I looked at my mother and
her face reminded me of the Virgin's with tears – wooden

too – that seemed to be clinging to her cheeks. When we were kids, Antón used to tell us that if we touched the Virgin's eyes, we'd be saved from all life's misfortunes. Catalina was always stroking them, and Javier, and Marco. But I never touched them. What if the lids closed and left me with my finger stuck in a Virgin's eye?

And the man laughs but I don't so much as smile.

'As the water of a lake dries up or a riverbed becomes parched, so he lies down and does not rise; till the heavens are no more, people will not awake or be roused from their sleep,' read Antón. And the thing is that I don't know what was going through my head at that moment, I really don't know, but you wouldn't believe just how loud I laughed. That explosion of laughter rose from deep in my belly and boomed out to the very edge of town. It was some laugh, sir. Then my sister, who has no notion of laughter or anything else, started to make a sound that we'd heard from her before, at home. Because at one time, sir, my sister used to make a kind of bellowing noise that I've always thought must issue from that empty space she has in her head. And she bellowed and I laughed. Everyone was alarmed and Marco stopped lowering my father into the grave, and when I saw the old folk, all shocked and upset by the weird sound Nora was making, I laughed even harder, the sort of laugh that makes your eyes water and you feel your stomach contract from the effort. And my mother, who was a Virgin at that moment, frowned at me so hard that I could read in her eyes the phrase she used to say when we were little, 'What a pair of laurels I've been given'. And no matter how I tried to stop myself, I laughed again and you could see my sister couldn't stop bellowing either. I think that's what death is too: uncontrollable laughter. Laughter that is born of itself. And then Antón said, almost screamed, 'Make them stop, this minute', in that priestly tone he uses to get on his high horse, to say I'm the one who knows, not you. That was when Javier took us away. And what happened after that stopped my laughter and made the burning return.

Javier and I are sitting on a bench in silence, not looking at one another; he has one hand on my thigh and Nora is beside us in her chair, with her wasted body and her loose jaw like a pail dropping down a well. That image, sir, has come to me night after night. And the thing is that it's an image that has been with me my whole life; it's a preordained future that I've always lived with and even desired. For many years I've longed for Javier – almost a shrub – and I – a strong tree – to sit that way, tired of saying 'I really like you' so often, 'cause in this town, what I've learned about love is exactly what I've learned about life: just how long-lasting feelings are. But at that moment, when time – I'm talking about the hands of the clock – was a mishmash of yesterday, today, and tomorrow, that image of the two of us with Nora made the burning return, and it flares up again whenever I bring that image to mind. And sitting on that bench, I began to understand that they were my end of the world, that what the people who knew the world was ending were referring to were those two people, sitting either side of me in some strange, timeless time.

I look into the forest and tell the man it's time. Time to lie to me. Lie to me, sir, tell me that my father is still hanging around here, that the dead stay with us and the gap they leave is nothing but a mist that soon evaporates. And, still looking at his feet, the man says convincingly that the dead do in fact stay with us and I thank him. The world, sir, has killed itself so often that it makes no difference now. I want to think that life breaks every one of us at some point. I want to think that some day a nanny goat will turn up at the door of my house and that goat will be my father. I want to believe that one night, wherever I am, I'll go to the kitchen for water and find my father there, looking at me. I want to believe that he'd have supported my decision to leave 'cause once, a few years back, when I dropped out of school, he said, 'Lea, set your sights far from here'. My father believed in the end of the world and the world came to an end for him. What I believe is that finding my father dead at our front door was one more sign that my life is not, definitely not, here.

SHEEP

The man and I have been sitting in silence for a while. I offer him my joint in case, now that he's got used to having the forest there in front of him, he might enjoy a smoke. The man wags a finger in refusal and I shrug, tell him not to worry. I can see he's missing his dog, but I don't say so.

I've got everything planned, sir. Tomorrow, on the second day of this new year, I'm going to get up and feed the chickens, but I won't open the store; my mother can do that later. I'm going to say goodbye to the goat and all the rabbits that are still running around the house. Then I'll load my things – I don't have much – into my father's car, a car nobody wants now, and I'll drive to Pueblo Grande; Javier will have already gone there to open the bar. I'll smoke some of Marco's weed; it helps me to stop seeing the forest, but I also need it to stop seeing Javier and be able to tell him not to look at me, tell him love and desire fizzle out, that my happiness lies elsewhere; tell him that I don't want to start a war 'cause wars always cause disfigurements and I like his body intact, tell him that I don't want to start a war, but I'm suffocating, my fire is going out, and I'll die if the rest of my life is little more than four streets, a grocery store and a church, and I've run out of I-really-like-yous, and trees die of grief, and I don't want to die waiting for him to decide to love and desire me, that love is something else; and I say that without any real experience 'cause I still haven't shared my love with anyone and my desire, my desire, my desire can't be a grape drying in the sun, and if he doesn't want my desire, someone else will. But what a pity, Javier, I'll say, what a huge pity that you didn't have the courage.

And then I'll go to see Catalina at the Jorge brothers' hatchery and hand over the envelope with the money I've saved so she can have her leg operated on, which is what she wants most in life. And I'll get back in the car and drive to the address Marco's given me. He's the only one who knows about it, the one who's helping me. Because Marco has always been fond of me, sir. And when I reach the city by the sea, I'll ask how to find the address I have, and they'll let me sleep on the floor of a house there.

Sleeping on the floor doesn't bother me; I don't need to know about comforts yet. Marco's organised it all.

Afterwards, sir, afterwards can be days, months, years.

Afterwards can be anything. Afterwards, what comes is life, sir, I don't mind being a runaway horse. Afterwards comes life. But I'll have got out of the world's end, you see. No, you can't really see. I'm ruminating, sir. It's true, I don't have many possessions, but I've packed pyjamas and a few photos, and I've taken my father's wedding ring. You can't imagine the trouble we had getting it off his finger. I've taken it as a memento and 'cause I know my mother will lose it sooner or later. But I won't. And I've also packed Nora's milk teeth; Ma kept them in a pillbox she took from Jimena's house when she died, so I'll be taking something of my grandmother and something of my sister with me. I don't know what to take of Ma or of Javier. Probably best to take nothing. When you leave this sort of town, there's no coming back.

I don't know how it is where you're from, sir, but when you escape from here, you don't return. We're cursed in this town. And the curse is a forest that has no way out and a mayor who believes in ridiculous conspiracy theories, but most of all the green of the woodlands. Here, people like to believe that the forest, the trees, are deadly, but that's 'cause they don't know any better. You see, sir – and I'll confess that I'm not one hundred per cent sure of this – I believe that the people who disappear in the forest don't die; they move on from the weariness of the countryside, of tiny towns, and reach somewhere else. And they find what they're looking for and renounce what they had. That's why we never see them again. But, naturally, sir, that's death too.

If I leave, I can't come back. You only have to look at what happened to Ana and Julio. I'll tell you their story, sir. The old folks used to tell it to Marco, Catalina, Javier and me when we were small and they'd always end by saying, 'Better the devil you know.' People are always saying that in this town. They say it to anyone who questions our way of life, to the people who come here from the city by the sea, to those who live in Pueblo Grande, to the man who drives the bus that runs twice a week, to the doctor . . . 'Better the devil you know'. And it may be true, sir, I can't deny it. But if I leave, I can't come back; the curse on this town isn't the forest that swallows up the lives of those who get lost, it's the evil that grows inside you from staring into that forest for so long.

Ana and Julio were a married couple from here and, like at our house, all their windows overlooked the forest. They had some land, but very little and not productive. They were well liked in town 'cause here you're well liked until you aren't. And one day Julio's brother called and said, 'Look, you and Ana should come here to the city, you'll thrive, you'll do well here.' And Ana said no, no way until she finally said yes from being bored by so much greenery everywhere. And, on the basis of that bad advice, they took their chances in a city, as so many people did around then. I'm talking about the time when people were moving away from small towns. Not a single local paid Ana and Julio a farewell visit before they left 'cause they were all indoors muttering, 'Shame on those who go away. Who's going to love them better than we do here? What they know is worthless anywhere else.' And when they left the house not a soul, not one single soul went to wave them off with a white handkerchief. And the point is that when they got to the city, they were caught in the poverty trap and Julio's brother died a few weeks after their arrival so that, with no work and no money, within a month they were yearning for the scent of dew on the grass in the mornings. Ana said, 'Julio, let's go back. Please, let's go back,' and Julio said no, no, no way until he said yes and in less than a year they were packing their bags to return. But you'll never guess what happened, sir. When the townsfolk saw them coming, someone said, 'Absence makes the heart grow fonder, but presence turns the fondness cold'. And they – Ana and Julio, I mean – feeling so relieved to be home, found an empty town where everyone was avoiding them.

One day Ana said to Julio, 'I must be speaking very quietly; when I ask the time in the square nobody answers.'

And he said, 'Ana, when I say good morning, they don't even turn to look at me.' The two of them were crying all the time, sir; crying from loneliness and bitterness when they sat down to dinner. And it seemed that everyone in town, absolutely everybody, wanted them to disappear; they were wondering how that pair could just come back as if they'd never left. Everyone was longing for them to disappear, they were clamouring for it, telling one another so in the stores, visiting each other just to say it, just to hate them for being deserters, the ones who left, the ones who abandoned the countryside and then had the nerve to come back. And that hatred, sir, reached Pueblo Grande, and people there began to talk about Ana and Julio too, and it's even said their resentment crossed the Pyrenees to the French Landes and crossed the English Channel to the south of the British Isles. Then, between them all, they cooked up a plan. One day when Ana went out for meat, she ran into two townsfolk and said, 'The forest is so leafy this year!' And they replied, 'What forest, señora? What forest are you talking about?' And another day, Julio was buying tools in the hardware store and said, 'You should see the forest! It's so green it'll change the colour of our eyes.' And the people in the store replied, 'What do you mean? There's no forest around here.' And in time, all the inhabitants of this world's end managed to convince Ana and Julio that the forest they could see with their own two eyes didn't exist and their dinners became ongoing discussions about whether or not what they saw from their windows was really there. They were so filled with doubt that the forest ceased to exist for them, and where the woodlands had been, they only saw dry countryside. Then, one summer's day, believing they were going for a walk in the open country, they entered the forest and it swallowed them like they'd jumped into the crater of a volcano. No one tried to stop them, and when they were sure they weren't coming back, they held a celebration, sir. They killed rabbits and rolled around in their hatred like pigs in mud.

Then a boy saw the light – I've always thought that we must be related 'cause if I'd been there, I'd have done the same. As he watched the whole town proudly rejoicing, he suddenly realised that an act of revenge had started a war. The boy got up onto a table and said, 'Can't you see, you sheep? Can't you see that you've killed them with your pettiness? Prepare yourself and your children because the forest has eaten without being hungry, and one day all the disappeared are going to turn up in our homes and bury us in the woodlands with them.' The people went on celebrating 'cause they thought he was just a kid talking rubbish and if he went on bothering them, they could dispose of him. They'd discovered that killing was easy, could be as easy as keeping up a lie. Better the devil you know.

Do you understand, sir? Do you understand that if I leave, in a town like this they won't want me back? The green of the forest has always scared the life out of me. The forest, sir, the forest. When I was a child I used to imagine there were deformed animals in there, monstrous horses with the faces of fish, starving cows with fox tails. I imagined that the tree trunks twisted around each other to make the paths narrower and narrower.

WHEN I LOOK AT YOU, I SEE

The man takes out his phone but the screen doesn't light up. I'd lend you my charger, sir, but I'm a mess and don't even know where it is. I'm always having to borrow Javier's or Marco's. You're missing your dog.

I don't know about missing things. I mean I only know about missing the dead, I tell the man. Not the living. I don't know what you feel or where you feel it. Because I've got a big heart but my love is short-range. Like Esteban's rifle, which has a long barrel but the bullet doesn't go very far. I'm the same, what I love is near at hand and doesn't move. And yes, I've sometimes wished my sister were like me. That she were a woman of her age, and with a regular head, not an empty one. True, I've missed something about her, but it's nothing I can change.

And I suppose missing is kind of like that: the desire for something. Don't you think so? You're missing your dog right now, but that's 'cause you didn't want it to get lost. Do you see? The point is that missing isn't something I've done much of in my life. And that makes me afraid of the future. That feeling might be so big I wouldn't be able to bear it. Or this might really be the end of the world, not a burning in my gut, or the death of a father, or a memorial card you don't want to look at. I don't know. Anyway, it frightens me. I'm frightened of missing.

Don't you think that love isn't, in fact, the same as being in love? That they are overlapping circumstances. And the man blushes, stops looking at me, and turns his eyes to the forest.

Don't be scared of me, sir. Like I said, if you want to put your head on my shoulder, I won't touch your face, I like happy people, not sad ones, and you have a sad man's face. No, don't get me wrong. I'm just trying to say that love isn't the same as desiring, as wanting. Desiring isn't important, what matter are the circumstances, the situation. Sorry, I'm ruminating again, sir.

There was a time when my sister could walk. That was when I was small, around five, six or seven years old. It wasn't quite walking; my parents would stand her upright, pull her, and her feet would react, first one moving forward, then the other. And when they took her out, my mother would always come home saying, 'Heavens above, this town has got long!' That was 'cause they went so slowly that this pitiful pocket of land we live in would become a megacity. But Nora would be radiant when she returned from those outings and her eyes would be so pretty, almost as big as open tulips. If I'm to be sincere, sir, I found it hard to understand that my sister was different. As a child, I'd often say to her, 'When you're able to play, I'll come looking for you.' And I feel I'm still saying it now we've both grown up. When I'm feeding her in the evenings, for instance, and then put her to bed, that phrase passes through my head, 'When you're able to play, I'll come looking for you.' As though at some point the world could be prepared for my sister. As if, sir. For my sister, the world killed itself the moment she was born.

When May came around, it brought cold weather we hadn't seen around here for at least two Januaries, as though time – and I'm not talking about the hands of the clock now – had gone mad, sir. You wouldn't believe the cold. My mother took out the thick wool blanket to keep Nora warm in her chair; since she never moved, the cold seeped into her bones. Life went by quickly for everyone. Didn't I say, sir, that death is just one day but life is many more? Well, life soon adapted to the circumstances. And we got used to my mother's swollen eyelids and Nora's loose jaw – since our father's death her mouth has hardly ever closed properly. And we've also got used to finding the odd rabbit behind the TV cabinet or under the beds. Life goes on, sir, and the emptiness fills up. And like I said, I keep guard on my sorrows to stop them escaping from inside me.

It was on a cold day in May when Catalina told me a secret. We were clearing the weeds that sometimes grow on the housefronts – a young person's task – and as Catalina's head is so often in the clouds and she gets tangled in her thoughts, I ended up clearing all the weeds while she twirled her skirt. Out of the blue, she said she'd been thinking that if it was true that the new man was going to set up a creamery for cheeses, there was no reason why she shouldn't ask for a job there. 'What do you know about cheese?' I said. 'The good things we have around here are the vegetables and the veal, it's the grass that makes the meat red.' And she replied, 'No, no, no way can I put up with the chickens any longer.' And then she started telling me that whenever she passed Jimena's house, she stopped and looked through the windows. And that's how she knew that the couple scarcely looked at each other. They didn't cuddle up close; if one was in the living room, the other was in the kitchen and vice versa. She also told me that the husband's name was Miguel, that she'd spoken to him a few times, and it had made her body tingle and her cheeks look like two peaches, and then she added, 'I don't know what's happening, Lea, but every time Miguel looks at me, I think of cantering horses.' Cantering horses, sir. Don't you think that's nice?

I won't deny it, sir; Catalina has always had a kind of unbridled love for older men. Even when she was very young, she used to say she had feelings for Antón, for the priest, sir, the priest. And so much going to church that year almost turned her into a prayer card. And a few years back, when she was just sixteen, she started looking after an old man from around here and said she was in love, said that when she was with him she forgot her limp and felt that she could run through the old guy's valleys like she did before her leg got burned. I didn't wait around. Quick as a shot, I was standing in front of that man and telling him straight up that if he laid a finger on my Klutzy, I'd get Esteban's gun and he'd be the one running through the valleys. We get a lot of that sort of stuff in these parts, sir; longevity sometimes leads to perversion, particularly in small towns, and if you so much as touch Catalina's shoulder, she's hearing wedding bells. After that she only had eyes for Marco 'cause in one of the summer festivals, when they were watching a firework display one of the elves – like you, sir, an outsider who comes here and leaves in no time – had arranged, Marco hoisted her up onto his shoulders so she could get a better view and when Catalina felt her body against Marco's strong body, she was wild with desire. Imagine it, a mimosa being caressed by an oak. But Marco didn't pay much attention to her even though she wrote him letters, poems and songs. Some evenings, when she came to the bar, she'd ask Javier to put on that song that goes, 'I'd like to invent a country with you' and dedicate it to Marco, but Marco would sit there all deadpan 'cause when it comes to thick skin, he takes the prize. And he'd go on smoking or drinking, or if he was really high, he'd get aggressive; it was only to stop Catalina wanting him. Just once, I stood up to him and said I was ashamed to see him trying to hurt us. When anything like that happens, he puts his forehead hard against mine, like a bull threatening a heifer, and presses and presses, but I don't flinch, sir, 'cause I know that, at heart, Marco wouldn't hurt a fly. Or that's what I want to believe. And on those occasions, I wake the next morning with a flower on the doormat of the house, or a bag of freshly dug potatoes still in their earth, packs of the gum I like, or, if he really feels bad, some weed for me to smoke alone while I'm looking into the forest.

'Catalina, what about Marco?' I asked. The Catalina-Marco thing was an open secret. Have you heard that saying, 'the best cure for unrequited love is absence and forgetting'? Well, Catalina took the last part of that advice, sir. 'What about him?' she replied. 'He doesn't even touch me and spends more time looking at his cows than at me. What Marco feels for me is nothing, zilch, empty space. My chickens feel more for me than Marco does. But with Miguel, on the other hand, I don't know, it's like I meet his eyes and cantering horses appear, and not just horses, Lea, but goats, sheep, rabbits and even zebras. Zebras, Lea. Zebras pass in front of my eyes when I'm with Miguel, and all those animals run wild, there are even ones I've never seen before.'

Don't you think that's nice, sir? When you feel an attraction for someone that way, that strongly, I mean. And then life goes and messes it all up. I figure you must know more about that than me; at nineteen, love is a valley with many rivers to cross. And when Catalina said that to me, my gut began to burn all over again. And she went on listing animals, and there were sparrows flying, and bears, roe deer, dogs, and cats, hopping frogs, all racing in the same direction, she said. My gut was burning, just like it's burning now, thinking of that moment when I realised that for me, when I looked at Javier, not a single animal went running by. Not a leaf stirred. Because what I thought I felt for Javier wasn't in fact love, it wasn't any-thing, sir. It was the prolonged affection of living together in a small town, the attention I wanted him to pay me but, in real life, never has. And love faded away, just like the world did that cold May. But of course I lied to Catalina and cheerfully said, 'Catalina, in my town, which is also your town, they call that love, and when I look at Javier, it isn't animals I see passing before my eyes, it's whole marathons of runners making the earth tremble!' And I exaggerated, like I always do when I'm lying. But Catalina stood there looking dumb and said, 'Just like in the song, Lea, "when I look into your eyes, words fail me."'

A few days after that I passed the newcomers' house with Catalina. The 'unloved and unwelcome' was still there on the whitewashed wall, though you could see an attempt had been made to remove it. I thought it looked pretty good. She, as usual, stood rooted to the spot and I, unwillingly, stood rooted with her. 'What are we looking at, Catalina?' I asked. 'Look. Look there,' she replied, and I peeked through a corner of the window. And I saw them, saw a bored married couple. A father holding a child of four or five in his arms and a mother sleeping on the sofa. And her blonde hair was mussed on the cushion where she'd laid her head. 'I guess they're bored, Lea, aren't they?' Catalina insisted. I shrugged my shoulders and it occurred to me that boredom can happen anywhere in the world, and they were already bored when they arrived in this town. The woman's untidy blonde hair caught my attention again. I had the urge to brush it. Or braid it. I don't know how to explain it, sir, something about that sleeping woman's hair affected me. And then

I noticed that Catalina was smiling, waiting impatiently to catch Miguel's eye and receive a smile in return. I tugged on her arm, but she said no, no, no way was she moving. So I walked on alone.

I spent the whole of that evening smoking weed with Marco in Javier's bar. You wouldn't believe how quickly my thoughts were flying. And I glanced so often at Javier, who was behind the counter, that Marco said, 'You'll wear him out. Try looking at me for a while.' But instead of racing animals, what passed through my head were imaginary conversations with Javier in which I say, 'Javier, I've been thinking that I want to leave,' and he answers, 'Where are you going to go? You've got everything you want in this town.' And then I answer him, 'I want to look at you and see horses,' and he says to me, 'What, Lea? I look at you and I see freshly picked thyme and bay leaf.' So, I say, 'When I look at you, I see something sleeping, an abandoned animal, tied up,' and he answers, 'You're the one for me, Lea,' and I say, 'Lies, lies, all lies. You've never said that to me, you don't want to love me, you wouldn't dare to love me.' And he says, 'But when I think of you, I see those colourful hydrangeas on the edge of town,' and I reply, 'Lies, lies, all lies. Let's suppose the end of the world is real, that it kills us, wipes out everything and we're not even dust, not even particles of dust, Javier, would you settle for me? Would you want to settle for a small house, a bar, and a Lea you don't really love?' The thing is that here in town, that's how love has always worked; people get together with whoever's nearest out of apathy, and they end up sitting at the dinner table without a word to say and walking slowly to put off the moment of getting home. That's why I'm thinking of leaving. And I pronounced that last bit aloud, sir. And Marco said, 'What?' and I said, 'What what?' 'What where. Where do you want to go?' 'Anywhere,' I said 'cause in my head, sir . . . well, in my stomach, the idea of leaving was still sketchy. But Marco heard me and the words stuck in his mind.

Three weeks or so after that, sir – almost June but with the weather still so cold that it seemed the seasons had set out to send us crazy – I was serving alone in the store. As you can see, this is a one-horse town, hardly a soul lives here, and the people who did their weekly shop yesterday buy bread and not much else today, and I spend my time checking my phone when there's a signal and I'm lucky enough to have some data left, or doing word searches, which I adore. So, on one of those gloomy, greyer than grey days, I was sitting with my pencil and puzzle book at around half past two, which is when I lock up and go to give my sister her lunch. By that time, my mother's already eaten and will be taking a siesta, probably crying. The thing is that I was so engrossed in finding the word 'pellet' in that letter soup that I didn't notice when someone came in, despite the fact that years ago my mother hung a wind chime just by the door so that we'd hear it if we were in the backroom. Anyway, that day I didn't hear it, and when a 'hello' issued from lips that weren't mine, I got an awful fright. I don't usually frighten easily, sir, but that day I jumped and my heart rate accelerated so much that for a moment I thought they'd have to drive me to the hospital in Pueblo Grande.

'I didn't mean to startle you,' said the woman from Jimena's house. And there was no time to put on my backcountry eyes, sir, no time at all. 'Cause the moment I saw the blonde hair – tidier now – on the other side of the counter, I closed my eyes and a foal cantered by. 'I almost didn't make it,' she said and I answered, 'Pardon?' 'It's nearly your closing time.' 'You're in luck, then,' I said. And with all my heart, I wanted to add, 'What a sad face you have, child.' She smiled her tight-lipped smile again and I asked what I could get her. And the woman produced a list that was so long I needed two boxes for it all. She even took the sweet rolls nobody ever buys.

I noticed that she had stubby fingers and short nails. My mother is always saying I stare too much, but then she also says that you have to take a good look at what's new. And I might know nothing about smells, sir, but I do know how to look. 'I guess you'll want me to help you with the boxes,' I said. 'Would you mind?' she answered.

And even though my expression was saying, 'Yes, I would mind, 'cause I've got a hungry sister waiting at home,' I told her okay, it was no problem. Before we left the store together, I went to the backroom for a moment and left her smelling the tomatoes that, like I said, have a really lovely scent in these parts. And I watched her from the backroom. She couldn't see me so I was able to look her up and down, noting how elegant she was; elegance isn't a quality people in this town tend to have. She was wearing boots that our roads would soon ruin and a blue shirt. I figured it was of some particular material, maybe silk, definitely not a mixed fabric, some material we don't wear here, something from somewhere else. And the fire appeared in my gut again and this time I didn't close my eyes, but in the area of my brain where the foal had cantered past it was now followed by a fluffle of rabbits, running and hopping, and I quickly shut it off – the thought I mean, sir – 'cause I didn't understand it.

We walked in silence to what had been Jimena's house and I stood by the graffiti while she rummaged for her door keys. 'We leave our doors open here,' I said, 'That way we don't have to look for the keys.' There was no reply. She left me alone in a glaringly white kitchen. On the floor, resting against a wall, were paintings of baskets of fruit and freshly peeled vegetables, still life after still life of dismal food, sir. 'Are those yours?' I asked, 'The paintings I mean.' From the other room, she said they were and I said my favourite was the limes in a wicker basket. 'By coincidence, that's exactly how my mother smells.' I started to feel a bit resentful, sir, 'cause at that moment it dawned on me that I'd never been inside the house when Jimena was alive. I don't know how my grandmother used to decorate her home or what paintings hung on the walls. I felt a little – not much – as though life was getting out of control. You probably don't understand, but the thing is that Big Lea grew up in that house and now there was nothing left of the ground my mother used to tread on and Jimena had lived with for so long. And my eyes, sir, oh my eyes went all backcountry when the woman returned to the kitchen with her son in her arms. 'Keep that child on a short leash; if he goes into the forest, he won't come back,' I said. I was surprised, sir, so surprised, 'cause that woman's eyes were strange too, she had backcountry eyes as well and I've never seen a pair of eyes as suspicious as mine. It almost scared me, and I said, 'Don't look at me that way.' 'It was you who wrote that on the house, wasn't it?' she said. I shook my head. Shook it a thousand times. I was ashamed, sir. Ashamed of myself. Even though I usually do anything I like, whenever I feel like it. 'Don't deny it, it was you.' I put the box from the store on the table and left without closing the door, and instead of seeing the road, what appeared before my eyes were a cantering foal, hopping rabbits and a herd of roe deer. All heading in the same direction.

ILL-BRED AND IGNORANT

After that, sir, we had a snowfall in the middle of June that kept everyone home for six days. And you can imagine how heavy it was when I say that all I could see from the windows was a white, white forest. Well, during those snowy days, we three women – my sister, my mother and I – were trapped in the house, spending the afternoons saying the names of plants 'cause that's a game my mother used to play with my father before his fatal fall. Big Lea would say Camellia and I'd answer Rhododendron; and so we'd go on: Acacia, Azalea, Daphne, Busy Lizzie, Petunia, until I'd say, 'Let's try trees, Ma, flowers are boring.' And then she'd start Birch, and I'd say Hazelnut; and so we'd go on: Holly, Chestnut, Whitebeam, Elm, until she said, 'Time to stop, Lea. Nora needs changing.'

Those afternoons dragged; four o'clock was just like eleven and eleven the same as four. I also had long conversations with Nora, telling her that I thought what I felt for Javier wasn't enough and that the animals running through my mind when I saw the blonde woman weren't cantering from love, as was the case with Catalina, but from something I still didn't know. My sister, who is moderate in her ways but can also be a wild animal, looked at me and let a thread of drool drip down her chin; she hadn't closed her mouth properly since my father's death. Have you ever tried to close a mouth that doesn't want to be closed, sir? It's like carrying concrete from one farm to another.

After three days with our bums as flat as pancakes from so much sitting on the sofa, there was a knock on the front door and I immediately realised it must be Marco 'cause he doesn't know his own strength and when he knocks on a door it seems like his broad hands are trying to break it down. Outside, he chanted my name the way he always has, 'Little Lea! Little Lea!' he called and, after a short pause, repeated 'Little Lea! Little Lea!' That's what people often do in small towns. Call somebody's name so they'll come to the door, I mean. My father used to do it to my mother when they were my age, give or take a year, and seeing each other. At that time my mother lived in Jimena's house. Her bedroom was upstairs and she used to keep the window open so she'd hear my father. And when he reached the square, my father would start calling, 'Lea! Lea!' And from inside, my mother would call back, 'Darling! Beloved!' And they say in town that hearing those loving chants made you think life was an eternal springtime. For my part, when I visit Javier, I call, 'Hey, Handsome!' That's what I sometimes call Javier when I want him to want me, but he never calls back, he never chants to me; he waits until he hears my feet on the doormat, opens the door, and says, 'What can I do for Little Lea now?' Marco, on the other hand, chants to me, but I don't want Marco doing that and, inside the house, I'm as quiet as a mouse.

Anyway, Marco knocked and from the kitchen my mother said, 'One of these days, that boy will bring the door down.' And I called out, 'What does the town dumbo want?' And since not even the snow can keep him indoors, he asked if I'd seen what was adorning our house. And so I asked what he was talking about and he said, 'Come outside, come outside and see for yourself.' So I grabbed my father's thick jacket, which was still hanging on the coat rack by the door, stepped outside and, like I was bowed down by the weight of the coat, my feet sank into the snow. I stood there in silence and Marco, with his reddened fingers holding a cigarette, sighed as he exhaled a cloud of smoke. The words 'ill-bred and ignorant' were written on the wall of the house, right by the door, near the window looking onto the forest. Ill-bred and ignorant, in black capitals. Would you believe it, sir?

When I was little, I never stopped talking at school and if I was asked to give my opinion, I always had plenty to say. The teachers were fond of Catalina, and when she looked at them with her puppy-dog eyes, with her don't-ask-'cause-I-don't-know expression, her it-wasn't-me or nobody-loves-me expressions, they'd put their arms around her. And when she started to limp and other kids used to make her run in the playground just for laughs, there was always a teacher nearby to rake them over the coals. For my part, I knew that people understand each other by talking, but when it comes to the ones who aren't people, aren't anything, the best thing is to treat them the way you do cows, with a whack on the rump to send them in the right direction, so I'd plant myself in front of them when the teachers weren't looking and say that a sleeping dog doesn't bite, but it might wake up one day, and those kids would laugh and then I'd really sink my teeth into them, calling them every name in the book, sir. One time I told a boy that his mother must be a broody hen but the only thing she'd managed to hatch was an egg like him, all set to be fried in a pan, and the boy – apparently, he didn't have a mother – cried a river – What am I saying? He cried the seven seas – and the headmaster, who was meaner than a junkyard dog, explained to me that what was going on in your head didn't necessarily have to come out your mouth, and, feeling less guilty about the boy than I was sorry for Catalina and her crying eyes, I cockily replied that when the Devil has nothing better to do, he swats flies with his tail, which is a phrase my father used to say when he was talking about the Dolores family, and life is curious, sir, but when I said that to the head, he retorted that my sister wasn't the backward one who couldn't move; it was me. And then he added, 'Those dimwit parents of yours haven't had much luck, with one backward daughter and the other an ill-bred and ignorant brat.' And though I do talk a lot, I know when to keep my mouth shut 'cause if I'd answered that stupid, good-for-nothing bullshitter back, my mother would have had to bear the cross of having given birth to an idiot and an 'ill-bred and ignorant brat'. And we'd already given the old folks in town enough to pity us for with my sister.

And after that day, nobody called me anything else. I never complained, but once, on the bus coming home, I asked Javier if ill breeding and ignorance could be inherited, if when we were parents, our offspring would be like that from birth, the way roe deer inherit the white patches on their coats. And he looked at me with a we're-not-going-to-have-children-together expression, but I didn't take much notice 'cause I was scared by the thought that I really was ill-bred and ignorant. And ever since, those words have echoed in my mind, but I've got enough character for three and I reject that term like oil does water. And seeing those words on the front of the house I shared with the woman who raised me and a sister who'd never had the chance to be educated made my stomach start to burn so hot I was seeing stars.

'Who did that?' I asked and Marco snapped back, 'Who do you think? The outsiders, of course.' When the blonde accused me of writing that message on her house, I should have said she was wrong, wrong, wrong, that I knew nothing about it and I should have donned that face Catalina had when she was young, that it-wasn't-me face. But instead I flew off like a wood pigeon. And now my home has an equally cruel one. I tried to rub it off, but it was clear that even the rain wasn't going to wash it away. Marco said, 'I know, I know what to do,' and I hurried after him through the snowy landscape. Almost at a gallop, we reached the place where your dog must be now, sir, where the dead hares are piled up, their blood-stained bodies almost frozen. Their faces were just like my father's in death and Marco, who lost all his scruples long ago, loaded at least ten of the ice-cold animals onto his back. Without a moment's hesitation, I began to pick up the hares that fell and we made our way to the door of Jimena's house.

'Those newcomers won't come out until the snow has melted, and just imagine the smell that'll greet them when the sun gets on the hares,' said Marco. And there, on the doormat, he dumped the dead animals. I won't lie to you, sir, I felt like giggling. But I held back my laughter 'cause that really would have been ill-bred. Marco lit a cigarette and then stubbed it out on the white stone just by the doorknocker. 'Let's see what they've got to say to that,' he muttered. My cheeks were frozen, but my eyes weren't backcountry then, sir; my eyes held a little anticipation 'cause it was as if the animals I saw cantering past when I looked at the newcomer's blonde hair were now dead on the doormat, just waiting to emit the unbearable stench of death. Though the truth is, sir, I can't smell death either.

Before I went back to spend another three days holed up in the house listing the names of trees with my mother, Marco and I came here, sir, to this very spot, to smoke a joint – Like I said, I often sit here to think 'cause it's shady – and I spoke to Marco about how well I'd been raised by my mother, my father, the countryside, and this town full of old folks, and I told him that writing unloved and unwelcome on the whitewash wasn't ill-bred, it was a hint, and I said that well-bred people alert others, point things out, 'cause you have to say it like it is and if life in this damned awful stretch of the planet has taught us anything it's that people leave 'cause they're no longer loved. And then I asked Marco, 'Just tell me, tell me who on earth would want to come to the world's end? The people who come here just want to take advantage, they're winding us up.' And Marco agreed, said yes, yes, I was right, until he fell silent and his cold breath almost turned to ice, and with equal coldness, he said, 'You can't leave this town.' He'd remembered the words I'd inadvertently uttered in the bar when imagining conversations with Javier and that 'I'm thinking of leaving' was bouncing around in his head and he'd spent every night since wondering about why I was going to go somewhere else when I was loved here, when no one here had stopped loving me.

We looked each other straight in the eyes, sir; that's normal for me – looking people in the eyes, I mean – but it isn't something Marco tends to do. The thing is that Marco's always had feelings for me. Then I asked, 'When you look at me, what do you see, Marco?' And he cracked his knuckles, the way he does when he's thinking, then clenched his fists and said that when he looked at me, he saw a girl with messy hair, and I said no, no, that wasn't it. When he thought of me, what was the image that came into his head? And he replied, 'I don't know, Lea. I think of you, and I think that if you asked me to, I could spend my whole life carrying dead animals on my shoulders.' I had no answer to that.

Love is always different, even though it presents itself in the same way. Don't you agree, sir? For Catalina it's a pack of animals all cantering in the same direction, for me it's words I can't get Javier to utter, and for Marco it's his shoulders carrying dead hares. Weird. But I said that answer was no use to me; that I couldn't find what I was looking for. And he repeated that I'd never leave here, that the things I know would be no use anywhere else. And it's strange, sir, 'cause I don't usually put much stock in what Marco says, but that ill-bred and ignorant on the house-front – it was going to take forever to wear off – made me feel kind of small. I looked at my hands and they seemed small, I looked at the forest and I felt as small as a fallen leaf; that's how small I was.

So I couldn't, really couldn't find the strength to tell Marco that what I know would have some use in other places, even in China. And that's all I know. Instead, I sat in silence, feeling a little woozy from the weed and allowing my thoughts to stray into dark places, into the evil forests of my mind, where I found myself putting a lot of stock in Marco's words, and his 'You're never going to leave here'. But I shook myself out of that mood and, putting one foot in front of the other in the direction of home, said, 'You really don't know what you're talking about.' And he answered, 'I know you have a sister who's about as much use as a three-legged donkey, a dead father, and a grieving mother.'

And the leaf lying on the forest floor that was me, that was my small body, raged at the awful truth behind Marco's words. Because, sir, you have to say things straight but when it comes to my family, I'm the only one allowed to do that and if anybody else tries, I can bite like an animal. Well, you won't believe how I reacted. He was still sitting here, and I went up to him, grabbed his hair – it's shoulder-length – and said, 'I hate you, hate you, hate you.' I called him an arsehole, a bullshitter, a layabout, a liar, a bastard, I told him that the ill-bred and ignorant should be on his house, that there should be pillows in his bedroom bearing the words ill-bred and ignorant, and banners hanging from his balcony saying, 'Here lives an ill-bred and ignorant dickhead'. I dragged him up by the hair until my arms gave out and he seemed as tall as the tip of a cypress tree, and then I pushed him, pushed him to the edge of the forest, shouting, 'Leave me alone'. And Marco, keeping his violent temper in check, 'cause he'd never do anything to me, shouted what I'd said a few minutes before, that well-bred people give hints, point things out, and while I was running home, he finally yelled, 'Your trouble is that you don't cry enough, you ill-bred, ignorant brat.'

My mother was livid and said I was getting my come-uppance. She pinched my arm – in this town, that's what's done to brats – and wondered what my father would say if he saw the stones of his house defaced by graffiti calling us ill-bred and ignorant. And I took my feelings out on my sister, who was just lying there, smelling of piss, 'Shut that mouth, you moron,' I griped, 'there aren't any flies around.' My mother's slaps turned my cheeks the colour of two ripe, red plums.

Don't look at me like that, sir, don't look at me. I went to my bedroom and typed a text message to Javier, a message that would reach his phone when the snow passed and we had a signal again. 'Let the world end, Javier', I wrote.

During the following three days of being stuck in the house, I was full of doubts, sir, full of doubts and thinking about our function as people and the obligations we have to those around us. And I had time to imagine what my life would be like if I wasn't here. What my mother's would be like if I left. And my sister's. I came to the conclusion that their world would come to a grinding halt if I went away. How would my mother cope with a child like my sister, all alone, caring for nine stones of dead weight in this house that would be – just like Jimena's had been for her – too big. So one morning, I came down to the living room and asked my mother exactly what my grandmother had done that was so unpardonable. I wanted to understand, sir. And she told me that Jimena was a bad woman, that when she was little her mother used to humiliate her for no good reason and when my grandfather died, she stopped talking and didn't even say a word when my sister was born sick. And when my mother said, 'that is unforgiveable,' I replied, 'Use the past tense, Ma. Jimena isn't with us anymore.' And the thing is that, though she says she hates my grandmother, my mother hasn't got used to talking about her in the past tense, and it's been years since she died.

'She gave me no help in bearing the sorrow of the new mother of a child like Nora. She didn't come to visit, it was me who had to take Nora to her and when she set eyes on her grandchild . . . you can't imagine, Little Lea, you can't imagine the look of scorn and revulsion Jimena gave me. You don't look at family that way, Lea. When I told your father how she'd behaved toward Nora, he wanted to go straight around and tell her just what he thought, call her an embittered old woman. But I held your father back and he put a dead rabbit on her doormat to make it clear we'd have nothing more to do with her.'

And that's when I realised, sir, that if I left, I wouldn't be able to return to this town 'cause my mother wouldn't forgive me. She'd never forgive me. She'd do to me what she did to her own mother: forget me, forget she'd ever loved me. 'Please, Ma, never stop loving me,' I said, and she laughed like she used to before my dad's fatal fall. And her laughter managed to shut Nora's mouth just a little.

Do you know a song that goes, 'the wide oceans might shrink to nothing, but your black eyes will never die, your cinnamon skin will always be the same'? And, with a slight smile, the man hums along. 'Hey, sir, you don't look like such a sad-faced man now.' And the man takes my joint and puts it to his lips. I look into the forest and laugh.

Well, that song, sir, that's the song my mother put on after our conversation; she spent her whole period of mourning, her missing my father, singing that sort of song, the kind they play here during the August Festival, *boleros* about everlasting love, about feelings that never die, like the folk in this town who might pass on but still linger in the memory of our four streets and a church.

When you get down to it, the life I can expect in this place, sir, the good side of a small place like this, is a sort of romanticism that I don't think I'll find where I intend to go. And, in fact, I understand the outsiders, I understand when a person is used to nonstop endings – 'cause when I imagine big cities, megacities, cities filled with lights, people, and possibilities, I think of no end of endings, brief love affairs, speedy forgetting, sensations immediately replaced by others, which is what happens when you live in a city – they might want to come to a town like this to see what it's like when things last. I don't know how it is where you're from, sir, but here, just as hatred lasts, other feelings also become so huge they're immeasurable and, sir, despite the boredom, the passage of time here makes us magnify whatever so much as brushes our skin. That's why Catalina falls in love with anyone who looks at her and smiles, why Marco loses it when someone scolds him for no good reason, and why Javier's silence endures an astounding eternity.

During those following three snowy days, sir, with that ill-bred and ignorant written on the stone, and Marco's words in my mind, I really thought I might not be capable of surviving somewhere else; I'd be like a polar bear transported to the forest we're looking into. And then there's my sister, my Nora. What would be in store for her, her muscles, her loose jaw if I went away? I thought a great deal about the responsibilities we have to the place where we live, sir, and I thought that going away and leaving the women in my life alone, shut up in the house, would be ill-bred and ignorant.

A SERVING SOLDIER

When the snows had passed, the ice soon followed 'cause the normal June heat arrived and gave us a bit of a break from the craziness of the seasons. On the sixth day, the sun began to burn again and when I got up in the morning, I looked out the window and remembered the dead hares outside Jimena's house. I waited patiently for the sound of frightened wood pigeons flapping their wings as they take flight, which means somebody somewhere has screamed, sir. And I was waiting for the newcomers' screams when they discovered what was on their mat. But I waited and waited and suddenly the clock struck eleven and still no one had screamed. My mother had left early to open the store – after so many days with the shutters closed, she was afraid some of her stock would have gone off – but was so weary by then of caring for my sister that she'd forgotten to wake Nora. And that's why, at eleven, instead of screams, what I heard was the creaking of her bones; you see, sir, when my sister spends a long time in the same position her bones complain. I went to her bedroom and she was lying there in those big girl's pyjamas, the pyjamas of a twenty-two-year-old newborn. And I thought of those words, 'Your problem is you don't cry enough' and 'I know you have a sister who's about as much use as a three-legged donkey'. Well, I suppose I must know about other things, but I don't know much about donkeys; anyway, those two phrases made the burning in my stomach flare up 'cause my eyes were used to the human being that was my sister, as useless as a vase without flowers. And filling Nora's wasted body with Marco's words, I looked at my sister differently and remembered, sir; I remembered how my father couldn't bear the shame of pushing my sister's wheelchair through the streets of this town. He couldn't do it, preferred to take her out after dark rather than put up with the neighbours' comments. It turned his stomach to see the looks of compassion, like when Antón said, 'You should attend church more often, we pray for Nora there.' Whenever the priest came out with that, after dinner my father would complain, 'What the hell has that moron got to say to us? More's the pity that he's put his trust in a nonexistent god.' And my mother and father gradually became less interested in Nora's life. Her world was reduced to promises that were never kept: Nora, I'll braid your hair this afternoon; Nora, I'll take you out to see the rabbits in the yard later; Nora, you can come to the store with us tomorrow; Nora, when I get back I'll clean the earth so you can put it in your mouth; Nora, I'll sleep with you in your bed tonight; Nora, I'll give you a hug, but not right now. And my sister's world was a constant tomorrow that never came, a 'this afternoon', a 'not right now', a 'later', a 'tonight'. Perhaps that's really the end of the world, sir; waiting for something that never comes, I mean.

And Nora was lying in bed 'cause my mother had forgotten to get her up and make her breakfast, and until eleven o'clock, it hadn't entered my mind that I wasn't alone in the house. Oh, my little Nora, you're so quiet, so still, there's more of the plant about you than the animal. And I put my arms around her torso and felt her chest against mine, and her face against my shoulder, and her eyes sharp as needles on my face. 'Norita, dear, you look so pretty on sunny mornings,' I said; I'm always telling my sister how good looking she is. And I stripped her to put on clean clothes and saw a body that was more developed than mine. Boobs that had been horizontal for so many years they'd almost fused into her crotch, shoulders so used to falling forwards they almost met in the middle of her chest, and freckles – my sister is really freckly, sir – that have so rarely seen the light of day they've lost any meaning for being on her skin. It's strange, sir, when I look at my older sister I see a body that, after a while, frightens me a little. But the reason is that since I don't allow myself to feel sorrow, fear takes its place.

Nora wore glasses once. The kind that wrap around your face like goggles. My mother went to the city by the sea to buy them. I went with her, sir, and that was one of the first times I saw the sea, the sea that belonged to us 'cause we're close enough to it that in August, and sometimes in September, if you stand really still for a while, you can feel the salt on your face. Later on, we got lazy and couldn't find the time to buy Nora new glasses and nowadays her eyes are bare and my mother insists that with so much looking, she can see a lot, but I say that with so much looking she sees very little. What can life be like for my sister when she doesn't understand it, doesn't know what to do with it, when she's an eternally newborn child?

Once, sir, when a new boy arrived in school – something that happened only rarely 'cause there aren't many new people in Pueblo Grande either – I pretended that I was an only child, said I had no brothers or sisters, and Catalina, who was standing next to me, muttered, 'You can catch out a liar quicker than you can catch up with a cripple.' And I looked at her and said, 'If you give me away, Klutzy, I'll say you're a bedwetter.' So the new boy thought that I had no sisters or brothers and, to be honest, sir, I thought that having a sister like mine didn't count. But that same day, when I got home and saw Nora on the sofa, smiling as I came through the door holding the flowers Jimena had left for me at the bus stop, I said, 'Here, Nora, they're for you.' And she made one of her joyful noises, 'cause when she was younger my sister made other noises too. And, sir, I had the feeling that she loved me. I like looking after my sister, I like caring for her 'cause when I was born she was already there, she got in ahead of me, and though it should have been her job to explain life to me, like older sisters do, I assumed I had to explain it to her. Although, when you come to think of it, what sort of life am I going to explain to Nora now that mine's all mixed up and I'm stuck here without wanting to be here? What am I going to explain when she doesn't know anything, doesn't know anything about living? 'Ma, does Nora love us?' I once asked. 'In her own way, Lea,' she replied.

Nora wasn't supposed to see in her fifteenth birthday, and that year was the end of the world in our home. My father worked less to spend time with Nora and my mother used to take her to the store 'cause she didn't, really didn't want to lose a minute of that last year of my sister's life. The townsfolk took their funeral clothes from their closets and kept them near their beds for when the bells announcing Nora's death rang out. Antón even had a special sermon ready and the mayor was planning a day of mourning. But my sister showed no signs of quitting the world that year, and on her birthday I could read annoyance on my parents' faces. 'How come you aren't getting out the rattle to celebrate Nora's birthday?' I asked, 'cause we always used to make a big racket that day as it was one of the only things she reacted to. They had no answer to that, but I'm smart and I felt that, deep down, they would have preferred her life to have ended. Not because they didn't love her – don't look at me that way – it was just the weariness of waiting for something that never happens, sir. That's all I know. And in the following years my parents went on breaking their backs while the doctor said it was quite possible, really quite possible that having reached that age, Nora could survive whatever life had in store for her. 'Obviously,' he said, 'she'll become progressively weaker, less mobile.' When Nora reached fifteen, I said to her, 'Nora, stay here with us.'

You see, sir, I was looking at my sister's strange body and I thought that Nora is really a vessel. Lack of air turned her into a ceramic vase. I mean she's a lifelong vessel. Because we – you, me, my mother, Javier and anyone else in town – digest our emotions and do something with them. But Nora just holds them, they don't seep into her, don't penetrate her, don't go anywhere, just like confused moles. Did you know that when moles get confused they can't even orient themselves by the smell of food? And they dig and dig and dig without really knowing where they're going. Well, that's how I imagine Nora's existence, sir. I imagine a small, blind animal tunnelling in the ground without knowing which way is up and which down.

When I reached fifteen, sir, the world didn't come to an end for me; it took a different form. I went back to telling Javier that I was into him, was really into him, using that special tone of voice I sometimes adopt when I want to make something true sound truer, when I'm stating something I consider everlasting, 'cause, though you might not remember, but when you're fifteen life is endless and emotions are like strips of chewing gum that stretch to eternity and don't even lose their flavor when you chew hard. Well, I was so serious about repeating just how into him I was that Javier kissed me on the mouth and his saliva stayed on my lips for days. And, with my eyes gleaming, I moved his hand to my chest, sir, to my boob – unlike Nora's, my boobs don't sag – and Javier kissed me harder and Esteban, who was in the square and saw our lips meet, called out, 'Every lover serves as a soldier'. And then we went to the empty house, I mean Jimena's; like I said, that house was a kind of lovers' hotel. Javier – a strawberry tree – and I – something different from a plant – lay on the bed in that house, and on that mattress Javier began to change into a willow with a stout trunk but weeping branches, the kind that almost reach the ground, and he played with my body so delicately that I – there's a lot of me that's animal – climbed up the Javier-tree like those squirrels they have in dry places. And, looking back on it now, despite the small scrap of love Javier was ready to offer me, I felt like the most desirable fifteen-year-old in all of Spain. All of Spain, sir. Even in parts of France. You can take it from me.

The man looks at me, but I can't figure out his expression. Don't look at me, sir, don't look. And the man – the tips of his ears have gone red – quickly looks away.

What I'm trying to say, sir, is that however little desire Javier might have for me, that evening, on that mattress, we made love for the first time, and then he went home to his house – his mother still hadn't disappeared into the forest at that time – and I went to mine. When I walked through the door, I saw my parents dozing on the sofa and Nora dribbling. My sister is one long oral infection. While I was cleaning her bleeding gums, doing my best to separate her upper and lower teeth, I told her all about that evening in Jimena's house. And I ended by saying that the world had changed colour for me, said that before it had been all dull colours, but now they were all so, so very bright. And I remember that on the June morning when I was waiting for a scream and studied my sister's wasted body, it occurred to me that she would never know love in that way. Pleasure. Do you see what I'm getting at, sir? She'd never experience it and a life without pleasure turns into a very steep mountainside.

'Nora, do you love me?' I asked for the sake of asking. And my sister shivered slightly from the cold. 'Don't shiver, Nora, I'll have you dressed in no time.' And seeing my sister that way, so vulnerable, so forgotten, lying so quietly in her bed, I realised that if my life was different, I'd go far, far away, sir. And I know some things: I know how to stack tomatoes and plums; I know where to place the bananas in the store to stop them going black so quickly; and I know how to make the chicken look more appealing, less scary. I also know how to plough the earth and milk the cows, and I could tend the animals and, if I put my mind to it, I could ring Antón's church bells, and of course I could work in Javier's bar. I've done that lots of times. I know how to change the nappies of a twenty-two-year-old woman, I know how to clean Nora so her backside doesn't get sore and how to give her massages so her legs don't swell. And I also know how to feed her and sort out her infections and give her the medicine when she has bronchitis, and how to quiet her before giving her an injection 'cause Nora feels them, sir; she spends so much time lying still that sometimes her blood stops, it just stops flowing, sir.

I know all those things, but that's all I know and my place is here. The idea that my mother might die while Nora is still alive frightens me a lot. But at that moment, with my sister so quiet in her bed, I understood that when my mother gave birth to me, she expected me to be alone with Nora at some point. It may well be that that some states can be inherited, and there's no escaping hereditary, so if Jimena was left on her own, maybe we should be too. It's hereditary, sir, in the genes or something like that, but I don't know about such things. At other times it occurs to me to wonder where I'd go when they haven't stopped loving me here. Javier may well learn to physically desire me or at least want to be with me, not from habit but from love. Love, sir, love is all I'm searching for and I have it here, I really do. So, convinced of that, I told Nora that, since the newcomers hadn't started screaming, I'd go along to bury the hatchet and hurry off with the dead hares. 'I don't know what to do about the ill-bred and ignorant, Nora; it'll probably fade or if not, it can stay there; it's better for the mistakes we make to remain visible as a reminder, so we don't make them again. But, Nora, who's going to take care of you?'

The man seems a little perplexed and I offer him another drag on the joint. Sir, have you cooled down yet? I ask and he nods. I'm telling you all this, I say, so you'll have something to talk about later, when you run out of things to talk about. And I need to get it all out 'cause otherwise it festers, and that's not so much pain as a sorrow, and what's the use of sorrows if you can't count them? The man looks at me and I think there's something tender in his expression, but I don't take much notice. Your dog's taking its time coming back, but don't let it get you down, I say, I'm sure your dog's smart enough to know that the hares around here are a one-day wonder. Then we both look into the forest.

When I carry Nora downstairs, sir, I'm always very careful. I put her arms around my neck and drag her down the stairs, and I do it with care, so she doesn't get hurt. That day, I brought her down to the living room and gave her some fruit. Then I left her watching that channel on the TV that shows music videos, just as the song that goes, 'Who, who is sailing my ship?' was starting and that seemed perfect 'cause at one point it says, 'Whatever you ask of me, I give it to you, give it to you.' The neighbour's dog was in the house again, moping around. 'Dog,' I said, 'stay here with Nora, and if anything at all happens, you bark.' Just like I did the day my father died. I opened the front door and there they were on the mat: six potatoes and eight carrots, still in their earth. Like I told you, sir, when Marco goes too far, he leaves his best apologies on the doormat.

I don't know, sir, don't know how to explain everything that happened next. I arrived in the square and saw Antón coming out of the church with his arms wide open and a smile on his face. He came up to me and I asked, 'What's going on, Antón? What's going on?' and looking up to the sky, he answered, 'Little Lea, I'm so foolishly happy.' And behind him I saw Catalina coming out, followed by her father – the alcoholic who hardly ever took her out of her cradle – arm-in-arm with Juana. I couldn't believe my eyes and Antón went on with his foolishly, foolishly happy stuff, so many years without a wedding and now we finally have a marriage here in town. And all astonishment, I went over to Catalina – she was wearing a short red dress – and, sounding distressed, she said, 'I don't know, Lea. I don't know about these things.' And right after that, Juana came up and said I'd been right, been right all along, it's always darkest before the dawn. And I still had no idea what was going on, sir. Catalina told me later that the first day we were all snowed in, her father ran out of drink and, in desperation, went begging around the houses for a swig of anything they had, but everyone refused him, said no, no 'cause none of them trust Catalina's father, sir; he sometimes gets the urge to set fire to things and once almost charred Marga from the pharmacy in Pueblo Grande when he was trying to burn some scrubland. So he went from house to house until he knocked on Juana's door and called out, 'Juanita, Juanita.' He thought that calling her that way, she'd open up 'cause it seems that was what her brother used to call her, and her eyes went all squinty with tender memories and she let him in. Apparently, she gave him beer and wine and they got talking and it seems they both adored that song, 'Now in silence, my love, I want to shed my tears' and then it was all: I feel such deep pain and mine is still alive, and I remember your wife, and I remember your brother, and I've got some wine, and I love wine, and why don't we dance, Antonio, let's dance. And then Juana put on 'I had a cat by the name of moon' and they danced real slow and she recognised love in his eyes, something she'd never felt before, something she'd never imagined would be part of her life, something that was for others, and in Juana's arms he recognised a forgotten love, something he thought he no longer deserved, something he thought he could only find in the bottle. And what had started out as a self-interested visit became six days of love that felt like at least a century. And he said, 'Juanita, if the world ends, I want to be with you when it happens,' and, with devotion in her eyes, she said, 'Yes, yes, yes, when the snow's gone we'll get wed,

I don't want to quit this world without having experienced matrimony.'

'I don't know, Lea. I don't know about these things,' said Catalina, and then added that she'd spent the whole six days at home alone and I thought that was all for the good, but I didn't say so, and Catalina's tears began to gush as she complained that if her father wanted someone to love, he could have chosen her. Laments like that get on my wick, sir, they set my teeth on edge, make my stomach burn, so, with a resigned expression, I snapped, 'When you've finished with the sob story, Catalina.'

Antón rang the bells to announce the marriage and the surprised townsfolk came to their doors to applaud and cheer. Viva! Viva! Catalina's father mopped his tears of joy on an embroidered handkerchief and the swarm of people around the couple were asking questions, getting out bread, and drinking wine while still cheering, Viva! Viva! But after a short while the men started going up to Juana and saying, 'Careful with that one; he can't hold his drink,' and the women warned him, 'Don't you go touching a hair on Juana's head.' My mother put together a small, improvised basket of fresh strawberries and plums, which are incredibly sweet in these parts, incredibly sweet. Then I snuck off to Jimena's house to remove the hares.

On my way there, I saw Javier, who was coming from the graveyard, walking slowly, as usual, with his hands in his pockets. He spotted me in the distance and turned in my direction. 'What does the handsomest man in town want?' I called. And he lowered his eyes, out of shyness, sir, pure shyness. 'Let the world end, Lea,' he said when he was beside me and I asked what he was talking about. 'The message, the text you sent me. You said let the world end, as far as I'm concerned it can end.' I could see he was nervous and looking pale. 'What's wrong, Javier?' Like I said, sir, Javier first shows his teeth, then leaves a mark, and he marked me in my loving eyes. 'What's wrong, Javier? What's wrong?'

Javier sat on a bench from where, out of the corner of my eye, I could just see the pile of dead hares on the newcomers' doormat, and when he began to speak, I was hoping they wouldn't come out and see them. Please, please, don't let them see, I was thinking. 'Lea, I believe the world may very well be ending,' said Javier. And I said, 'What are you talking about? What?' And he said, 'Yes, let it end. You know that a nanny goat that was my father appeared in the house, well now it's my mother. I've been alone there with her for the last six days.' And my eyes darted straight to Javier's face, with its straggly beard that makes you think there are patches where not a single hair grows. Like in the countryside, sir. Have you noticed that there are places in the countryside without any trees at all? Because that small patch of earth doesn't allow roots to grow, well that's how the handsome Javier's cheeks are. 'I don't know what's going on, Lea, but I swear to God that my mother – the woman who left and never calls, the woman they say went into the forest, though I've never wanted to believe that – has been in the house with me for the last six days. And if I wasn't sure before whether my mother had passed on, if I'd thought she'd left and didn't want to come back, I know for certain now that she's dead, Lea, 'cause this morning, when I went to fetch the car to shoot over to the bar – it's been closed so long I won't be able to cover this month's bills – a newborn foal was curled up on the doormat. And, Lea, I'm not going to give you the foal 'cause though I wasn't interested in having the nanny goat around, I do love my mother. And so there she is, tethered with a piece of the twine used for tying bales of corn 'cause I had nothing stronger. In corners of the darkened house, I often used to think I caught a glimpse of my mother, wearing the same clothes as when she left, the same shoes. I used to talk to her as though she'd never gone away, but this morning she *had* gone and that little creature appeared.' 'What did you say to her, Javier? What did you say?' I was dumbfounded, sir. I thought he was a bit crazy, that being cooped up at home had done something to his head, and so I said, 'Javier, it's probably just the stress of not being able to open the bar.' And he answered, 'No, no, no way, Lea. The world is coming to an end and I believe my mother has come to tell me.' 'Exactly what did you say to her? Just what did you say?' 'Well, I asked if she'd come to stay, if she was dead or alive, if she went into the forest, if she was real or just one more disappeared watching us in the night. And there was no answer, not a single answer, Lea, not a change of expression, not a smile, she just blinked slowly.'

Do you see what I meant, sir, when I said that in this town the dead don't leave us, that they stick around, linger? And the man thinks that over, thinks it over and looks up at the high treetops.

'Anyway,' Javier went on, 'When I saw that foal, Lea, it reminded me of when my mother disappeared, and I turned a deaf ear to what they were all saying 'cause I didn't want to believe she'd gone into the forest alone. Who'd want to get lost, to die? But she did, apparently that's what my mother wanted. And since I kept saying no, no, no way is my mother dead, no post was planted. But now that I understand the forest swallowed her, I've been to the nameplace to plant a post for her, and I've carved a foal's head on it. If the world ends, it ends, and my mother can rest in peace. And, to be honest, with the shortfall this month and everything coming to an end, what do I want a bar for? Thank goodness I found you here, Lea. You're always here when I come looking.'

You're always here when I come looking; it was the prettiest thing Javier had said to me in years, sir, in my whole life. And what I'd thought when I was studying my defenceless sister lying in bed seemed even truer. Love is what I'm searching for and I have it here, I really do. 'When you come looking for what, Javier?' I asked. 'When I come looking in general, when I come looking for anything, I find you.' I smiled at Javier and without thinking, came out with, 'When you think of me, what do you see?' And Javier said, 'I don't know, I see Little Lea, the same as always, the girl who's forever calling me handsome.' 'Come on, follow me; this world isn't dead, it's crazy,' I said. And as we walked the short distance that separated us from the newcomers' doormat, with the townsfolk still celebrating the weird marriage of Catalina's father and Juana, I had time to remember what Esteban said on my fifteenth birthday: 'Every lover serves as a soldier.' And, sir, it may be true, it may be that love is not giving up on an idea, like what I told you about Ana and Julio and the sheep that led them to the forest, maybe love is not giving up on an idea.

'Will you give me a hand with this?' And as Javier isn't one to ask unnecessary questions, he started to load hares onto his shoulders, just as Marco had done a few days before. We were each picking up as many of the dead animals as we could when Catalina appeared and, all wide-eyed, said, 'What are you up to?' 'Collecting this stuff, obviously,' I answered. 'What a pair you are,' she said. 'And what are you doing here?' 'I've come for Miguel.' That's when I understood that the red dress had nothing to do with the wedding; it was to look good for Miguel – the newcomer, I mean. 'And the chickens?' I asked. 'I'll see to them later. And anyway, after six days, they'll all be frozen.' 'Well, let's hope they're alive and kicking 'cause otherwise what are you going to do?' 'Miguel will give me a job in the creamery.' Javier gave a small, a minuscule laugh and Catalina said she didn't know what was so funny, claimed we never took her seriously, we had something against her, were always underestimating her; the usual stuff. And there was some truth in what she said, sir, 'cause Catalina's like a weather vane, always changing direction with the wind, and if that saying about there being no smoke without fire is true, I can tell you, sir, she's always smelling non-existent smoke in that wind.

While Javier was loading the hares, I said, 'Catalina, don't do that. It'll be just the same as what happened with the Dolores family, they'll eventually exploit us. Can't you see that those city folk come here all full of themselves, with their vibe of 'we know best and you're just hicks'?' 'No, no, no way, Lea. These ones are different. I like Miguel and he's said he'll teach me everything and I'd prefer to know about cheeses than chickens, plus he'll pay me better.' And Javier said, 'Catalina, he's married with a son.' 'You don't understand, Javier. You don't know it, but they came here 'cause she had an affair, she was cheating on him, and she doesn't really love her son. Hardly ever touches or dresses him. She doesn't like him, doesn't love him. And they've come here to make a fresh start, but he can't do it, he just can't, he says something has died between them. But of course, he has to try; for the child, for the child's sake.' 'And where did you hear all that, Catalina?' I asked with a frown. 'He told me, and the stuff about her not loving her son came from Marga and Marcela 'cause they've seen that sour-faced woman through the window. Whenever they pass the house, their eyes stray and as the blinds are never closed, they look inside to see what's going on, out of curiosity, you know. And they've told me that she never even kisses the boy.' Javier sighed in resignation and I was on the point of saying all that was rubbish, that you should take a good look at yourself before passing on gossip about others, when at that moment the door of Jimena's house opened and the blonde woman appeared. I went stiff as a board, sir, and some animal started cantering across my mind again, but this time I was able to identify the emotions a little more clearly and there was fright, curiosity, and even some admiration. And don't look at me, don't look at me that way, sir. That's what I felt.

'Water can wash away anything but a bad reputation,' Catalina muttered, but loud enough for the woman to hear. And, not taking my eyes off the woman, I said to Catalina, 'Shut your mouth, Klutzy. You don't know what you're talking about.' The woman came outside with the child in her arms. 'See, just look at the way she's carrying him, it's a disgrace.' 'Shut it, Catalina!' And Javier smiled at the woman and said, 'Good day. I hope you survived the storm.' That's what we say around here when we get a bout of bad weather. The woman gave a smile and, putting on my backcountry eyes – just a little, not too much, sir, 'cause there are times when you can't avoid rage – I went up to her and said, 'It was you who wrote ill-bred and ignorant.' And she looked at me with a serious expression, a very serious expression, sir. 'Lea, that's your name, isn't it?' And I didn't move a muscle. 'The next time you come to leave something at the door, try knocking. It's ill-bred to come to a person's house without saying hello,' she said and then added, 'Do you mind?' indicating that she wanted to get past me. I could have felt guilt or anger 'cause she'd seen the pile of dead hares, but what I did feel was the burning in my stomach; there was something in the tone of her voice, her gestures and the way she moved, something in everything about her, sir, that told me she hadn't been responsible for the ill-bred and ignorant. I can't tell you what it was that made me so certain, but she hadn't dirtied her hands writing on our housefront.

Then, when the blonde woman had almost reached the church, Catalina rang the doorbell and Miguel came out. I noticed the way he looked at her and the truth is that Miguel really did find Catalina attractive. You can tell, sir, when an older man has the hots for a nineteen-year-old girl, and I don't know how you feel about it, but I have to confess that it makes my stomach churn even harder. I noticed the way he looked at her and knew he was thinking of getting her panties off and without wasting a second, before the two of them could move away together, I went up and – trying to copy the manner of his wife when she spoke to me, that stuck-up, citified way of speaking, so unlike our small-town way – said to him, 'Miguel, that's your name, isn't it? You're going to explain all about cheeses to her, aren't you?' He nodded and I think he said something else but, to tell the truth, sir, I can't remember what. 'I hope that when you're tired of the cheese, you don't start thinking of breeding pigs 'cause in these parts we slaughter them.' And when he was about to ask what I was getting at, the neighbour's dog began to bark real loud, the way I'd taught it. I didn't have time to tell him not to lay a finger on Catalina or get her hopes up, or hurt her in any way. Instead I grabbed Javier's hand and said, 'Come on, Nora must have had a shit.'

And hand in hand, the two of us walked by where the townsfolk were still celebrating the wedding, and Catalina's father was singing, 'My little girl is so pretty, so pretty when she's asleep,' and I slowed down so that Javier was the one tugging on my arm now, as though letting me know we had to hurry to my house 'cause the dog was barking, but I stopped to listen to Catalina's father, surprised by the strangeness of the whole scene. You may not understand, sir – I don't know, don't know your opinion – but for me it was strange to see Catalina's father looking happy. And Esteban's words about lovers being serving soldiers came back to me. That's what Catalina's father had been, a serving soldier with a dead lover, incapable of even caring for his little girl, the apple of his eye, 'cause he just couldn't, sir, he didn't feel capable of it. But don't run away with the idea that I'm trying to justify how little attention he'd given his daughter, no way: I condemn it.

When we got back to the house, there was nothing wrong with my sister and I gave the dog a good scolding, 'No frights, dog. No frights. The last time you barked my father was dead.' Then I said to Javier, 'See how lovely my sister is. Help me get her into her into her chair, will you?' And between the two of us we got Nora settled. 'Every time I see her, she looks worse, like a dirty napkin that's gone stiff,' said Javier. 'How would I know?' I answered,

'She seems the same as ever to me.' What I didn't tell him, sir, was that she was indeed getting to look more like she had cardstock for skin by the day. We took Nora with us to Javier's house, with him pushing the chair up the steep streets and occasionally coming out with some reproach like, 'What do you feed this girl?' or 'I wonder just how much Nora weighs,' or 'Lord, I don't know how your mother manages her.' 'Habit, Javier,' I said, 'We've spent our whole lives carrying her up and down like a dead weight, we're used to it.' We were going to see the foal that was his mother, the mother who always loved him, the mother who chose the forest, the mother who maybe felt as trapped as I do in these four streets, a church, and a general store. His mother, who was now a foal, was also a serving soldier with a dead lover, 'cause she had two loves die on her: Javier's father and the man who was afterwards Javier's father, who, when he died, was a nanny goat that Javier never wanted, never loved.

I can tell you, sir, that when I saw the foal tethered with that thin twine, something in its way of looking reminded me of the woman who was Javier's mother. The thing is that Javier's mother wasn't like mine – she has a darkish complexion and tired eyes; his mother's eyes were slanted at the corners and somehow passionate. I'm not saying that my mother has no passion for life, it's just that she bears a weight that Javier's mother never knew.

But my mother is passionate about small things and she radiates the beauty of someone who still has dreams to fulfil. I don't know what they are, sir, because she never talks to me about that. Well, anyway, the foal had those slanted, passionate eyes that seemed to be saying I'm not afraid of anything. And it's true that when she looked at her son, she radiated love. Like I told you earlier, sir, Javier's mother used to come to help mine and since she often went to the city by the sea, she once told my mother that she'd found a good place for Nora. She meant a care home or something of the sort. A place where Nora would be with people who weren't her family.

Ma and Dad never liked the idea, although I do remember them talking it over one night. 'Think about it, Big Lea. I'm just asking you to think about it; it might give us a break, she might be happy there.' 'Don't talk rot; if your daughter's going to be happy, she'll be it with us. And just what is that woman insinuating? That my daughter isn't well cared for?'

I do believe, sir, that now time has passed, and Nora is more a woman than a child, Ma regrets not accepting the offer of that woman who is now a foal. Because otherwise, she'd have had more time for fulfilling the dreams that are still in her eyes, the dreams she doesn't mention to me, and most of all I think my sister really would have been happy there. The foal looked at Nora and I was longing for the animal to say something to me like, 'This girl is dead to life'.

I don't want you to get the idea that my sister is a burden, a load, sir. No, no, no way; Nora is the light of my life, but her light is dimmed by a veil. I'm only trying to say that for my family, the weariness of being unable to do anything for her happiness has slowly worn down our souls. That's all it is, sir. And the man looks at me and smiles. And I look into the forest.

'Lea, can I kiss you,' asked Javier after observing his mother for a while. 'In front of Nora?' I responded nervously. I was really nervous, sir. 'I don't think she cares,' he said. I looked at my sister, whose jaw was hanging loose again and who was looking at us. 'Go one then.' And Javier kissed me on the mouth, here, more on this lip than the other. And, once again, his saliva stayed in my mouth for days. I blushed as red as the evening sun. That was acceptance, sir; a kiss from Javier with Nora dead to life, his mother tethered with a piece of twine, and me with a burning in my stomach that I guessed I'd have to get used to 'cause Marco was right; I can't leave this place.

THE MOST FEARFUL MAN
IN THE WORLD

Javier started asking me for a kiss more often after that. The following evenings in the bar, even when he was serving customers and we were at our regular table at the far end of the room, I could feel his eyes on me as if, with the foal still in his house, he'd suddenly realised that he had some sort of feelings for me. I allowed myself to be kissed by the handsome Javier, sir, 'cause he'd had my heart in a vice since I was small, and for a while I put the idea of leaving on the back burner. It was enough for me to feel the tenderness he was beginning to show, and I was foreseeing a life spent with him and Nora, thinking that the boredom would be easier to bear with Javier carving wood beside me. To tell the truth, that more than anything else seemed to be a sign that the world was going rapidly downhill 'cause, if I'm honest, Javier has never had any feelings for me. But I let myself go with the flow, settled for kisses that were getting hotter.

On those evenings in the bar, we all seemed to have changed. Catalina was crying less about the death of the world and wearing short skirts and blouses that had belonged to her mother, stuff her father had always hidden so she wouldn't even smell them. But since the wedding, he hadn't set foot in the house with its stale smell, the smell of windows never opened, and was living with Juana, who had recovered her youth to the extent of shaking off the scourge of being Juana, Julio's sister, and become Juanita in her own right. So Catalina was living alone in that stale-smelling house and she opened the windows every morning to fill the town with that song that goes, 'My heart aches from loving you so much'. Catalina is sappier than the poetry they made us read in school. Anyway, now she was proudly wearing her mother's clothes and Marco was drinking more than we'd ever seen him drink before and by the time the evening was coming to a close he'd be embroiled in an argument with some idiots from Pueblo Grande that always ended in a fight. At first, sir, I'd separate them, until one time I was trying to sort out the problem and got a nasty blow to the head. No one was ever sure if it was Marco's fault or the person he was brawling with. The day after, he – Marco – left weed just for me on the doormat and around twenty packs of my favourite chewing gum. So, for the first time in months, or even years, the picture we painted at our regular table was different. Although by late July, Catalina was in tears again.

Esteban – the man who killed my dog – was known in town as 'the most fearful man in the world', and that, sir, goes back to when he was married and had a son. A son who'd now be a little younger than my parents. What happened was that Amparo – his wife – decided to pull out some plants that were growing on the housefront 'cause Esteban said that those creepers were so dark, they were giving him nightmares. The plants were black as black can be, sir. So one morning, she left her little boy Estebitan playing with the wet sheets hanging in the yard and started removing the plants. And that evening at dinner, Amparo said she had a strange feeling in her legs and not long after it spread to her arms and then her throat. 'I can't breathe, Esteban! I can't breathe!' she said to her husband, but Esteban didn't even have time to ask what was wrong before she dropped dead on the floor and Estebitan started playing with his mother's skirts. Esteban was so paralysed by fear he couldn't even touch his wife. And for many minutes he was kind of stupefied, rooted to the spot, his eyes wide as saucers, fear filling every inch of his body, until a neighbour came to the door and saw Amparo with her face all red and her hands all green. Green as death, sir. She was taken away and later some men from the city by the sea turned up in town to remove all the plants of that black colour, which it seems make people drop dead in a matter of hours. But in fact they couldn't find hide nor hair of the creeper on any of the other houses. The turmoil went on for months, sir, 'cause Amparito was much loved and the neighbours never ceased to comment that if Esteban hadn't been so afraid, his wife might have been saved. And the gossips began to say that although he was now a grown man, Esteban still suffered nightmares that made him wet the bed, that he was even afraid of rabbits, of swallows, and of tall trees. 'Esteban is the most fearful man in the world', someone said.

After that, when he'd got over the upset, Esteban tried to prevent anything so much as touching his son; No way was the child going to suffer the same fate as his mother. He used to carry the boy around with him everywhere, wrapped in a sheet strapped across his chest. His plan was to track down the thing that had killed his wife, so, with the child on his chest, he prowled around the edge of the forest, his eyes on the ground, 'cause he was convinced that the poison came from the woodlands, and whenever he saw some new plant with a strange colour that seemed to grow differently from others or had leaves pointing in the direction of his house, he shot it with his new rifle, making Estebitan cry.

Eventually, sir, life became an uphill struggle for Esteban as he started to fear things that aren't the least scary. Not a day passed without him being frightened by the speed of cars or of hares. And as he was a bit trigger-happy, he used to kill dogs, thinking they were wolves. Like he did my dog, sir. 'You'll end up killing your son,' they told him, so his greatest fear was of himself and his inability to put his rifle down. He soon gave up on his search for the poison ivy and, with the gun always resting by the door, dedicated himself to raising Estebitan, who was growing taller and taller.

When Estebitan reached puberty and a hair almost as black as the creeper that had killed his mother sprouted on his chest, they took to calling him 'the least fearful man in the world' 'cause, in contrast to his father, he wasn't afraid of anything and thought so little of his own safety that everybody said he'd end up suffering some mishap. He lived his life as though it was charmed. When he was eighteen, he attempted to carry on his father's search and for a time he'd take up the rifle and shoot at the undergrowth, but the problem was that as he wasn't afraid of anything and none of those plants looked poisonous to him, and after ten minutes in the heat of the August sun, he'd be back home complaining that it would kill them before the forest did.

Estebitan had so little fear that the town soon became too small for him and one day, after he'd had enough of the sun, he said to his father, 'I'm leaving, I'm going. I'm off,' and he was so bent on getting out of town that he loaded the car with his belongings and left with his dog Lima, without a cent to his name, heading for the city by the sea. It seems he must have run out of petrol, or his battery died and, disoriented, not really sure if he was going back the way he'd come or was headed in the right direction, he set out walking with the forest on his left, and he kept walking on with the idea of reaching some inhabited place, but as nobody knows we exist, as we're the world's end, not a soul passed along the road and Estebitan, his mouth dry by then, continued on for hours until his awful thirst made his saliva thicken to the point where he couldn't produce any more and his face and whole body started wrinkling like a raisin. He refused to try to find water in the forest 'cause when death appeared at his shoulder, he began to fear everything, even his beloved dog Lima, and when the sun had almost turned full circle, he fell down dead with half his body in the road and the other half in the forest. Lima came back some time later and, as though the dog had told them every last detail of the story, the townsfolk went out looking for Estebitan. They found him with his lips white, sir, and no one ever really knew what had happened. I believe the story I've just told you, word for word, 'cause I like to think that the least fearful man in the world was afraid of death, but there are people who say that, having so little fear, he ate some treacherous forest fruit and – just as happened to his mother – stopped breathing and dropped dead. On his headstone they wrote, 'Estebitan, the least fearful man in the world.' Though I always think it should have been, 'Estebitan, the man who was only afraid of death.' Esteban was grief-stricken and for a couple of years his heart beat so loud you could hear it all across town. I wasn't alive then, but that's what they say, that it was beating loud with loneliness, with despair.

And, sir, it was despair that brought Catalina's tears back. What happened was that at the very end of July, Esteban – who'd already shot himself in the foot on the day my dad died – was arriving home from tending cattle, with his usual stern face, when he noted that his heart had passed from beating loudly to not beating at all, and clutching his left arm and crying oh, oh, oh, he collapsed on his own doormat with his eyes wide open. Miguel, who was coming back from the creamery with Catalina in high spirits at his side, immediately ran to Esteban's aid and said, 'Don't worry, a doctor will be here in no time.' And crying her eyes out, Catalina said, 'The doctor only

comes through here some Fridays and today is Tuesday.'
So Miguel, feeling kind of overwhelmed by it all – I guess
he was wondering how he'd ended up in this corner of the
planet – went to fetch his car. Esteban, who was still able
to speak, said, 'I'm afraid, afraid, so afraid,' 'cause despite
all his unhappiness, he still wanted to go on living. And
Catalina, who's fonder of misery than a miser his money,
spent the whole journey to the nearest hospital repeating,
'Holy mother of God, it's one thing after another. Our
world is coming to an end.'

They left Esteban in the hospital and as soon as the
news got around back in town everything was prepared
for when they would be informed of his passing. Javier
spent his nights carving the coffin that would shelter him
deep in the earth, Antón ordered a headstone that would
be placed between Esteban's son's and his wife's and had
it inscribed with, 'Esteban, the most fearful man in the
world.' The thing is, sir, that not much happens in small
towns, so when we know something is going to happen,
we like to have all the loose ends tied in advance. Well,
time passed without news of his death. On the tenth day,
cool as a cucumber, Esteban reappeared in town, all rosy-
cheeked and a few pounds lighter. 'Do my eyes deceive
me?' said Antón when he saw him crossing the square.
'You can't kill a weed,' said Esteban with a smile. 'What
do you mean, weed? We don't see many oxen as strong as

you in these parts.' 'Your God gave me the health that my wife and son lacked,' said Esteban, shouldering his rifle to go to tend the animals.

In fact, Catalina wasn't crying from the shock that Esteban gave us all; it was 'cause, when she and Miguel were driving him to the hospital, what with the tears, the upset, and the stress, she went and kissed Miguel full on the lips. And in spite of the fact that, when it came to Catalina, his only thought was how to get into her pants, and he'd been filling her head with pretty words and looking at her honey-eyed, talking about the creamery, he backed off and played the decent family man.

Sir, I could have been cruel to her again – you already know how her tears were getting on my nerves; I could have said, 'I told you so, Klutzy, but you never learn. This must be the fifth, sixth, seventh, eighth time something like this has happened to you, but, stubborn as a mule, you just go on singing the same old tune, with the same old flood of emotions. Let's see if this time you learn that love knots up your feelings and that the unknotting kills you like a runaway car, like an angry sea.' I could have said all that 'cause I'm smart, sir, and though I might not know much about love, I know all those things just from observing, just from observing others. But instead, I said, 'Catalina, when men are more like filthy pigs than baby lambs, they don't know which way the wind's blowing and they have absolutely no dignity, no principles. You're too much of a woman for him, you have a life that he lacks, and I already told you that he was the sort of man who sweet talks you and touches your bare leg, but is then jumpier than a cat at a loud noise.' I told my Klutzy all that 'cause disillusion had returned once again to her life. And at that moment I realised how much I admired her, realised that there were no limits to Catalina's determination to love and be loved, and her memory is short-term. It makes no difference how many times she's been rejected, how many times Marco has said no, no, no way; Catalina has looked for love in many men and none of them have wanted her yet, but she's held out, she hasn't given up, she's found a way to pick herself up and keep loving just as strongly as the first time her eyes felt desire. I, on the other hand, have only had eyes for one man and though I've had other options, which if I'd chosen them could have allowed me to feel wanted, really loved, or at least to learn about desire and the heat of intimacy, time after time, instead of following Catalina's example, I've chosen to bang my head against the same brick wall, against that gigantic wall that is Javier and his ridiculous belief that, out of the blue, he loves and wants me. And you see, sir, I'm not even satisfied with having him. And that's why Catalina's persistence made the burning in my stomach return so strongly that for a moment I thought

I was going to throw up there and then on the table in front of everybody. And the reason the burning returned was that I was thinking I had to get out of this town. 'I want to leave here,' I said again, out loud. And I think that since I wanted that from my gut, my mouth failed me, and against my will it opened and let out my voice. As Catalina was crying loudly and making other noises, she didn't hear me, but Marco did and this time he just gazed at me; gazed and gazed at me.

After that, what made people go back to feeling that the world was killing itself was that Esteban went from being the most fearful man in the world to being Esteban, the man death can't touch. You see, sir, after the heart attack, in the space of less than four weeks, all sorts of bad things happened to him. First he had some kind of stroke that almost left him like Nora, and well you might ask how we'd have managed with another like my sister in town. Then he broke both wrists trying to get his rifle out from between two rocks, where it had fallen. And, to top it all off, he fell out the window of his house when he was scaring off a swallow that had nested on the roof. And between all that, his heart showed signs of stopping at least three times. He had us all on the edges of our seats, and Antón was constantly planning masses 'cause we all thought Esteban was going to leave us. One day, Marcela went up to Juana and said, 'Just as well you got married, life is coming to an end for us this year, and no one can deny it; you only have to look at Esteban.' And, feeling worried about Esteban, the mayor came to visit us for a couple of days and, shaking his head, said, 'I'm just praying that it doesn't hurt, nothing more.' Only the blonde woman seemed bewildered when townsfolk talked about the inevitable end and, in astonishment, said, 'The things you have to listen to,' and then she carried on with her life as though that terrible event wasn't going to happen.

THE WORST PIG

The man stands up, says he needs to stretch his legs and I think he's going to leave. Don't go, sir. Don't go. And there's a please in my tone that I don't utter 'cause it isn't needed; by now the man is afraid of the forest. He looks at me, experiences a moment's doubt. He's questioning his love for his dog, you can see it in his face. But he looks toward the forest then turns to look at me. The man trusts me. He believes that if he keeps waiting, his dog will come back. Patience is a virtue, sir; at your age, you must know that. And if life has offered you this chance to rest here beside me, take it. The man looks, and looks, and looks at me. Then he sits down again. Thanks, this story will soon be over and you'll never see me again. Never. And afterwards you'll be left with the memory of your dog getting lost, just that. And perhaps in a few years you'll tell this story to somebody and you'll find some moral in it, like in the fables they read us in school. Like in songs with stories. The man smiles. See, I say, you're cheering up a little.

'Nora,' I said before we went to bed, 'Nora, I'm trying, I'm willing myself to want to stay. Step by step. And I tell myself that if the countryside is full of imbeciles, who knows how many fools there are in the cities; I tell myself I'm fine here, that I'll stick with my own imbeciles. Why meet new ones? Better the devil you know, isn't that what they're always saying in town?' I paused, sir, 'cause when you want to convince yourself of something, pauses are really important, but I'm always saying what I think the moment it crosses my mind. But truths can conquer valleys, sir; did you know that? And even if I did my utmost to convince myself that the holy grail of happiness is to be found in these four streets, truths are there to be told.

'Nora,' I went on, 'if anyone had to die, it should have been you. But life isn't logical. And I'm coming to terms with that. Step by step. And I'll tell you something: if I stay, what I want is for my life to be as short as can be.' At that moment my mother, who'd been eavesdropping, said, 'If you leave, take me with you.' And after a weird silence when time seemed to lose all meaning, I burst out laughing. My mother didn't laugh, so I said, 'But how can you come with me?' 'Take me with you,' she almost pleaded. And I laughed again and Nora was watching as usual, her eyes open wide as saucers. And Big Lea had a bitter expression on her face. 'Take me with you, Lea.' And my laughter made the cats in the yard run and hide. But my mother's lined face insisted, 'I mean it, Lea. If you leave, I'll feel all alone here,' and then she started to laugh too 'cause laughter is contagious. 'And where am I going to go, Ma?' I demanded. 'Nowhere, I hope. Our family's what it is, there's no changing it.' That thing Marco says about me not crying enough crossed my mind and that idea was like an attack of heartburn. I tossed and turned all night, sir.

When she's in love, Catalina wakes the whole town with the joyful music coming from her windows. But the following morning, she put on a song that wasn't cheerful: 'Don't be surprised if I say you were ungrateful, unthinking with my poor tender heart.' She'd taken her time about it, sir, 'cause weeks had passed since Miguel refused her kiss on the lips, all the time that Esteban had been teetering between life and death. And one thing I may not have told you about Catalina is that the first thing she does is to cry until she's dry as dust, but then she expresses her annoyance, her pain, her sorrow, her joy, in such a way that everyone, including the Tudanca cows upstream, knows just what our Klutzy is feeling or has stopped feeling. So, one way or another, the whole town has ended up giving her the attention she didn't receive from her dead mother. 'The child's got the music on at full volume,' said Big Lea when I came down for breakfast. 'Catalina's fallen in love again,' I told her. And, without taking her eyes off the piece of fruit she was peeling for my sister, she responded, 'Swan feathers for the battles of love.'

It was my turn to open the store that day and I walked there in a heat finally appropriate for the season. My arms were bare and the first mosquitoes had already bitten me. In this world's end, sir, there might not be much else, but in summer we have mosquitoes by the shedload. And the bites were stinging as I raised the metal curtain and switched on the lights. I started arranging the tomatoes while I was waiting for the bread truck to arrive – it had been turning up almost two hours late since the snow-fall – and it seemed a long wait. From inside the store, I saw Catalina heading in the direction of the newcomers' house but I lost sight of her when she turned the corner. She's never on time for the chickens, I thought. What a girl, what a girl, what a crazy girl, I mused, and fetched my puzzle book, turned on the radio my father had given my mother years back, and waited some more. I didn't see Catalina retracing her footsteps at a much faster pace, as Antón said she returned.

Thirty or forty minutes later, I saw Marco outside the window making funny faces and gestures and all, sir, like a small child. He does that sometimes, when the hot weather arrives, and sometimes, when he has free time, he comes to the store and we share a cigarette at the door. I stub it out the minute I see any townsfolk approaching or my mother; she once spotted me smoking with Marco and said, 'I'll die before I see you kill yourself.' Anyway, I went outside and said to Marco, 'What are you up to, you loafer? Smoking in store doorways never earned anyone any money.' and he said, 'Here, Lea, look, see what I've got.' And he produced Esteban's rifle from behind his back, and I gave Marco a look with my backcountry eyes, sir; he's the most backcountry thing ever. 'What are you doing with that?' 'I'm shooting at clouds to see if they break up,' he replied, pointing the gun at the sky. 'I've stolen it from Esteban. He's so busy trying to decide whether to live or die that he leaves it lying around all over the place and I found it propped up outside his house.' 'Give it here,' I said, 'I'll put it somewhere safe. You're the devil himself with that in your hands.' And like a little boy, Marco complained that I never trusted him. 'How am I supposed to trust you when you're such a blockhead, Marco!' And he said, 'That moron Javier's the schlump, now he spends the whole day wanting to kiss you.' 'What's it to you?' I retorted cockily. 'Well, he isn't being honest, he's lying, he kisses you 'cause he's a bitter man who has no experience of anything but the boring life he leads. There's no blood in his veins.' I had to laugh a little, sir, 'cause even if I was drooling over the handsomest man in town, there was some truth in what Marco said. 'If you were half as interesting as Javier—' 'Ah, give me a break, Lea; you don't have to look at him for more than a few seconds before you're saying you want to get out of here.'

Marco was winding me up again, sir. Where would I want to go when I'm loved here? If Marco is right, how can I go, leaving my sister behind? And, as he's always a bit too sure of himself, Marco pointed the rifle at me, sir, and it wasn't fear I felt but shame. 'Cut it out. If you end up killing me, what will you have to say for yourself then, Marco? What?' 'I'll say I've done away with a liar.' Then he lowered the gun and added, 'Javier might make your cheeks go as red as beetroot but, as you know full well, there isn't a person in this town who knows you like I do.' and then he stroked my face and I was almost more afraid of that caress than the rifle. The thing is, sir, Marco scares me, I'm scared of him touching me; I don't like it 'cause his hands are rough and when he held me back so I wouldn't see my father, I could hardly breathe. I brushed his hand away from my face in disgust. 'Lea, lying is ill-bred, ignorant.' 'That description fits you better; even the cows don't respect you unless you're carrying a gun.' When Marco was about to respond to that, we saw the newcomer approaching us, this time with her blonde hair tied back with an elastic band. Marco slipped the rifle under his shirt and I thought, 'That boy is so dumb, he'll shoot himself one day,' but the woman's words interrupted that thought.

'Who's been writing on our house this time?' Neither of us responded. 'I said, who's been writing on our house this time?' she repeated angrily. 'Cool it, blondie, you're spoiling your good looks.' 'Shut up, Marco,' I ordered. She fixed her eyes on us like she was drilling into our minds. 'You think you're so smart, but you don't have the first fucking idea.' The first fucking idea, sir; language like that didn't go with her citified face. 'You're a bunch of ignorant meddlers. Next time I'll report you.' 'Who are you going to report us to? You don't have the first fucking idea about small towns.' And Marco took a step toward her. 'And you,' she said, nodding at me, 'with nothing to say for yourself, you're even worse. Do you think I didn't see the dead hares you left at my door? What do you want? What do you want? What the hell's eating you?' 'And you? Just what brought you here?' I finally said, 'To take advantage of us like all the other outsiders? To eventually take our land? In this town, we don't welcome people who aren't loved in other places.' 'What do you know?' she retorted. 'I know how to scrape a living in this small town and I know we don't want people like you here; you outsiders only bring us problems. And that's all I know.' The blonde woman turned to go and when Marco made as if to follow her, I held him back 'cause Marco can be a wild dog if he's not kept tied up. 'It was Catalina,' I told him when the newcomer was almost back home. And at that moment I understood she'd also been the one to write ill-bred and ignorant.

I closed the store, put a sign on the door saying 'back in five minutes,' and Marco and I went to see what was adorning the newcomers' house now. And to be honest, sir, Catalina hadn't written any lies 'cause Catalina doesn't tell lies. 'The worst pig ate the best acorn,' Marco read aloud and laughed. 'There's a pig living here! A pig!' he started shouting. And I hissed, 'Marco, Marco, hush.' But doubled over with laughter, he said, 'That fool has no idea whose heart he's broken.' I went over to look through the window, the way townsfolk do when they're snooping, and I saw the blonde woman, who'd just arrived home, arguing with Miguel. He was waving his hands about and, in between glancing at his phone, he pointed at the woman, pointed at the child, and then pointed at the woman once more. She was pacing back and forth, shaking her head.

Then Catalina suddenly appeared beside us with a mix of anger and sadness on her face. 'Don't give us that woebegone look,' said Marco, 'The whole situation is funny.' And Catalina asked what he was laughing at, but before he could reply, I butted in with, 'It was you who wrote ill-bred and ignorant on my house, wasn't it?' 'Well, you are,' Catalina countered. 'And what are you? An acorn?' 'Yes, Lea, I'm an acorn; the best one, and he's a pig, just like the rest, all talk; they go filling my head with ideas and then it's no, no, no way. Like you said, I'm too much of a woman for him.' And Marco began to call out, 'Miguel, Miguel! In these parts, we slaughter pigs, we slaughter them!' 'Shut it, Marco. You're just as much a pig as he is,' Catalina spat out at him. And then Esteban turned up and said, 'What's all the shouting about?' and seeing his rifle poking out from under Marco's shirt, he added, 'That's mine.' And Marco answered, 'You're so forgetful, you'll leave your head on the doormat one of these days, Esteban.' Esteban was about to speak, I imagine to come out with something like 'A good thief hides his spoils,' which is something he often says, but he bit his tongue and just held out a hand. When Marco was passing over the rifle, it accidentally slipped from his grip – which was weird, sir, 'cause Marco's got a grip like a vice – and in the fall the butt hit a rock, and it seems that as Esteban hadn't used it since he wounded his foot that day my father died, there was still a bullet in there. The sharp impact with the rock activated the trigger and the rifle went off. Catalina, Marco and I were deafened by report and the shot hit Esteban straight in the chest.

Do you know just how much blood we've got in our bodies? It's incredible.

I know about animals that have been bitten, cows with bloody sores on their legs, and about skinned rabbits, but that's all I know, sir. I know nothing about blood gushing from a person's body. And when I saw it pouring out like spilled milk, I couldn't help but think about how much blood we have in our bodies and wondering if my father still had blood in his veins, there in his grave. And that reminded me of when he used to say to my sister, 'Nora, your blood is all clogged up, so we have to pinch you to make it move around.' Catalina and Marco don't know anything about blood either.

Immediately after the deafening shot, Catalina screamed and within seconds a number of neighbours had surrounded Esteban, who was lying on the ground with a hole in his chest. The newcomers also appeared to see what was going on and the blonde started saying, 'What have you done? What have you done?' And, in the turmoil, Miguel touched Catalina's shoulder to calm her – she was still screaming, and it was to quiet her, sir. I had my eyes fixed on Esteban 'cause his lower lip was trembling and, in his shock, he attempted to get up but when that failed, he said in a weak voice, 'I can't, I can't, I just can't.'

And I recalled my mother at my father's funeral, when she reminded me of the wooden statue of the Virgin, and now Esteban was reminding me of the Jesus figure with his crown of thorns that Antón has over the altar, 'cause, though the blood was coming from Esteban's chest and not his head, his eyelids were drooping in the same way. Catalina's father said, 'A doctor, a doctor! Someone bring a car, we have to get him to a doctor.' And Juanita grabbed hold of my mother and said, 'Oh, Big Lea, Big Lea! The end of the world is taking us one by one!' And I stood there as still as a post in the nameplace, and Marco, sir, he was paler than Esteban. He had his arm outstretched as though he was still passing the rifle to Esteban and his parents, who were also there, put their hands to their heads and wailed, 'My son, my son! What's my son gone and done?' And I said, 'No, no. It was an accident,' and Ma shouted, 'Get yourself back home to your sister!' And I replied, 'Really, truly, it was an accident.' But then the blonde – the newcomer – said, 'Look, just look what they've written on my house. It was them, they're evil, evil.' The bitch was accusing us. But the townsfolk were already keening for Esteban, and that reminded me of the day at school when they told us that Rosalia, the superintendent, had gone away and wasn't coming back, and everyone in class began to cry 'cause we were so fond of her. Then I looked into the blonde's eyes – without my backcountry gaze this time, but with every morsel of truth I possessed – and it wasn't wild horses that were cantering across my mind, but the dead hares I'd removed from her doormat and I thought so many things, sir, so many things, and I was so furious that for an instant I felt like biting her and saying, 'What do you know? You didn't see a thing,' but inside, my inferno of a stomach was telling me, 'Get out of town, get out of this town, get right out of this town.'

Esteban was taken to the hospital and they say he was pronounced dead on arrival. But he can't have been very dead 'cause two days later he was back in town and when he appeared in the square the neighbours gathered in a huddle to observe him. And you'll be wondering, sir, what kind of luck a person has to survive so much. But apparently the bullet had entered and exited without doing much damage, and only perforated this bone, here in the chest, without touching his heart or lungs, and it was as if his back had been warned in advance of what was going to happen, 'cause the curvature of the spine he'd had since childhood saved him from being bedridden for the rest of his life. Naturally, sir, so much coming and going between life and death affected Esteban's head, his mind was wandering, and when he got back to town, the first thing he said was that he'd survived 'cause he'd tamed the forest, he'd spent so much time shooting at the shrubs that the forest had decided to keep him alive until the world killed itself.

The mayor turned up again to witness with his own two eyes the dogged determination of Esteban's body to live. And with his arms open wide, he made a path for himself through the others and hugged Esteban in that sort of man-to-man way you all have, slapping each other on the back. Then he said, 'You're a walking miracle, Esteban, a walking miracle,' and he turned to the crowd with his uncrowned king air, his air of river that runs to the sea, to say, 'Ladies and gentleman, this shows that the end of the world wants us alive.' And Catalina, Marco, Javier and I viewed the whole scene from the bench by the entrance to the graveyard, looking toward the square with half-closed eyes because the bright sun was shining directly in our faces. 'Between the forest and this mayor, there's no hope for us,' I said, but none of them answered, or turned to me, or even smiled.

After the shooting, Catalina went back to the stale-smelling house and we didn't see hide nor hair of her until that day when she came to sit with us on the bench. Marco's parents had kicked him out and he'd spent the previous nights with Javier and the foal that was his mother in their small house. Big Lea wasn't speaking to me and she used to turn Nora's face away whenever she tried to look at me 'cause with so much going on, I'd also forgotten to be back at the store for the bread delivery and the town didn't have so much as a crust for days.

Sitting on the bench, while the mayor was making his dumb speech about the end of the world, I began to think maybe, just maybe, he was right and the end of the world consisted of nothing more than staying alive time after time. And that made me think of my sister; she stays alive even though she's dead.

And it's then, sir, at that point in the story – in early August, when I'd accepted that the fire in my stomach was the price I had to pay for laying aside the idea of leaving town – that I started to believe the world really was coming to an end. My characteristic laugh, that in the past had emerged every time I heard someone talking about the end of our days, had disappeared; I couldn't find it inside myself. But the truth is that the end of the world had nothing to do with Esteban's thousand deaths, or with Javier's sudden loving feelings, or Marco's gentleness after the accident with the rifle – he went from being a bull to the delicate person he was as a child – or how, after falling out of love with Miguel, Catalina started covering her scar again; what it had to do with was my home, the forest, the forest, with the belief that Nora was in fact my end of the world, an end of the world in herself. 'It's stopped loving us, Lea. This town has stopped loving us,' Marco finally said.

YOU'RE A MISFORTUNE

When people saw one of us in the street, they'd disguise their disapproval under coughs and I even heard muttered words like contemptible and wicked, sir. My mother said that business at the store – not great at the best of times – was lower than ever when I was serving. And though that didn't last for long, this small town took against us. 'It's 'cause they believed that blonde newcomer when she said we were evil,' I remarked to Catalina one day. 'I was right when I told you they'd only bring trouble.' And Catalina, who was like a light bulb about to blow since she'd gone back to hiding her limp, murmured, 'Unwelcome, unloved, piece-of-shit mum, piece-of-shit bitch.' Javier was the only one of us absent when Esteban was shot but, as usual, sir, he said nothing and if Catalina's tears had me at the end of my tether, Javier's sealed lips were beginning to get on my nerves too. He was in no doubt that it had been an accident, sir, and, what's more, he'd willingly given Marco a home, but I'd seen just how much blood there is in a body, and was certain that Javier didn't have a single drop in his. 'Your problem, Javier, is that instead of blood, you have thick honey in your veins and that's why you're so slow to answer, why you're such a clam.' And Javier looked at me and laughed and his laugh melted me like ice-cream on a hot day. What was bugging me about Javier was the way he hardly ever came to our defence. I was hoping he'd ask me for some empty fruit crates from the store and pile them up the way Marco did with the hares, and there, in the middle of the square, jump up on top of them and shout to one and all, 'Hey you fools, it was an accident!' Because that's what I'd have done; but, well, that's not his kind of thing.

The point is that time was passing and people weren't changing their attitude to us, not even my mother, who was still punishing me with her coldness. And while I said it didn't last long, in fact it continued through the whole of August and part of September so, looking back, it wasn't such a short time after all. But all the same, for me that month and a half flew by 'cause the person who took centre stage wasn't me but Nora, who, as though she weren't my sister, started doing the weirdest things.

First it was the tablecloth, sir. One evening – spent with me looking at Nora and my mother turning her head to the side so she couldn't look back, and me moving so she could see me – I felt I'd had enough and said, 'So, tell me, Ma, exactly what has offended you so much?' 'Just what are you thinking of, writing insults on the new-comers' house whenever it takes your fancy?' she said. And from the bottom of my heart, sir, I answered, 'What a relief! You're finally talking to me.' 'What's written on our wall is going to turn out to be true; you're ill-bred and ignorant,' she replied. I lowered my head. 'If your father were alive, Lea, he'd take you out of the store and make you plough the land with him.' And I retorted, 'But Dad's dead and we've been left alone, and just the thought of living in this house for the rest of my life is torture, Ma.' And my mother got up to pinch my arm, and all the while she was pinching hard I held back the tears brimming in my eyes, ready to fall, sir. 'Stop that, stop it now! It's your other daughter you should be pinching to make her cry, not me, not me,' I said, like I was trying to tell her that I could let my tears flow whenever I felt like it, but I'd been raised to believe that it was other people who cried, not us. 'If I were to start crying, Little Lea, if I were to start, we'd have an ocean outside our door instead of a forest.' And she let go of my arm 'cause Nora had hooked one of her stiff fingers into the tablecloth and was tugging with all her might. Everything ended on the ground; her plate shattered, the beans rolled away, her fork disappeared under the table, and the meat knife was embedded in the floor just by Nora's foot. 'What's got into you, Nora? You don't move in years and now you go and pull everything off the table. You're a total misfortune,' my mother cried. She left everything as it was and went to her room, where we were still finding rabbits under the bed. I looked at Nora, sir; I was shocked, thinking that maybe she did have some form of existence inside her, that there was somebody in there. But like a newborn baby, Nora simply moved her mouth and dribbled.

And then a few days after the tablecloth incident, sir, Juanita came to help my mother with something, but the thing is that I'd left Nora all neat and tidy in her chair, I'd braided her hair 'cause, after I accepted that I had to stay in this town, I started keeping the promises I made to my sister, and a perfect braid was falling over each of her shoulders. I left Nora there and went to spend the evening with Marco and Catalina in Javier's bar, and when I got back home that night my mother was in a state and told me that when she and Juana came back indoors from feeding the chickens, they found Nora lying on the living room floor with a gash on her forehead caused by hitting the table as she fell. 'I don't know, Lea, I have no idea how it happened. Your sister can't move her legs without help, so just how did she end up on the floor?' And then she added, 'It must be your fault. You can't have strapped her into the chair.' 'Or yours for not checking.' I snapped. But I'd swear that I did strap her in, sir, I know I did 'cause when you do something regularly – as you should know – when you do it regularly you never forget to do it. Anyway, Nora had a lovely bump on her forehead for days.

And on another morning, sir, when it was my turn to get Nora up, I went to her room as usual and in the half light, the first thing I did – the first thing I always do when I wake my sister, except when it isn't a bath day – was to open the closet, take out clean clothes, and leave them on the chair so they're ready for after her bath. Well, I did that and turned to see if the bed needed straightening, but Nora wasn't in it and for an instant, sir, I had one of those premonitions that don't make any sense and I was asking myself if Nora was so small she'd got lost in the sheets. But that idiotic doubt vanished quickly and I began to wonder if I'd got the day wrong and my mother had already seen to Nora, or if my eyes were unable to see in the darkened room. So I went to open the blinds and there I found her, sir, lying at the foot of the bed in her summer pyjamas, her eyes wide open, looking toward the window. 'Nora, who left you there on the floor?' I asked, without expecting any reply. The whole situation was odd 'cause Nora never moves a muscle at night and had never fallen out of bed before. And what's more, if my sister had fallen, she'd have bellowed, like she always does when something bothers her, and we'd have heard. I went to get her up and asked, 'Norita, how on earth did you get there?' And I mulled that over the whole day. Had something happened to my mother? Something must have for her to leave my sister just lying there on the cold bedroom floor. I found myself mentally grumbling about Big Lea, saying to myself 'She's always complaining about the pair of laurels we are, but I could say that too; some laurel of a mother I've got, leaving Nora on the floor and not even picking her up.' I spent the whole day long turning that over in my head, and when my mother came back while I was washing the nanny goat – Javier's father, that is – I called from the yard, 'How come you left Nora lying on the floor, Ma?' And she said, 'What do you mean?' She insisted that she hadn't, wondered how I could even imagine such a thing, said that if she saw so much as drop of spittle, she wiped it away in an instant, she would never leave Nora lying on the floor. 'That's where I found her this morning, Ma.' 'Well, it must be your fault, Little Lea, you're so wrapped up in your own world you didn't even realise your sister had fallen.' 'And how is Nora going to fall, Ma? She can't move and she bellows whenever something bothers her!' 'I don't know, I don't know,' she repeated. And I said to Nora, 'What weird things you're doing!' And at that moment Catalina turned up and, as she'd heard my words, she asked what had happened. 'My sister has taken to pulling off tablecloths with knives on them, falling out of her chair, and throwing herself off the bed.' 'Wow,' said Catalina and added, 'Heavens above, heavens above. It's like our neighbour who said the world was ending 'cause his cows were acting strange.' And I stared at her in disbelief. But Catalina went on, 'And your sister is more animal than human, Lea. Oh, the end is nigh and I'm still without anyone to love me the way I want to be loved.' 'Give it a rest, Catalina,' I said, 'What do you want?' 'Nothing, it's just that I'm home alone and I get bored.' I looked at my sister, wanting to ask, 'Nora, are you doing these things 'cause the world wants to kill itself?' But instead, I noted the fire in my gut flickering up, and my stomach always burns when there's a decision to be made. Don't forget that, sir.

That wasn't the last of it, not by a long shot; those things were trivial in comparison with what happened later, sir. One night, my mother was giving Nora dinner and I was in an armchair, glued to my phone, exchanging texts with Javier, who was telling me that Marco was feeling very low, he was crying. I have to say, something I've always liked about Marco is that despite being a raging bull, he cries well when he has to cry – unlike Catalina, who has waterfalls for eyes. When Marco cries, he doesn't hide his tears, not like the tough guys in this town who've made us believe that real men don't act that way. And Javier was telling me that when Marco got up in the mornings, the pillows were soaked and when he was cooking, his tears fell into the food. 'I don't know what else to do.' 'You're so slow off the mark, Javi, I'm pretty certain you haven't actually done much so far,' I wrote. And all of a sudden, sir, my mother yelled out to me and, sounding really alarmed, said, 'Lea, Lea, come here! Your sister! Your sister!' And I said, 'What's up? What's up?' And what was up was that Nora was biting her tongue hard, and her tongue was poking out between her teeth, staining them red with blood. I quickly pinched her arm to make her open her mouth to bellow, but she wasn't going along with that. 'She'll bite it off, Lea, bite it in two!' wailed my mother. And I said, 'Nora, Nora, look at me! Stop that!' But Nora closed her eyes. And, sir, there was no way we could force her jaws apart so I flew like a bird to Javier's house and said that my sister was biting her tongue and, since we couldn't separate her teeth, she was going to cut right through it. I was surprised to see Marco so gentle – like the hare he was as a child – and he came home with me and, using all his strength, opened Nora's mouth. While he was doing that, I stroked my sister's arm and said to Marco, 'Careful, be very careful, Marco.' We put antiseptic on the cut on her tongue and I said to my mother, 'This was your fault, you must have given her something to eat that confused her.' And my mother said, 'Or yours, misfortunes occur while you're looking at your phone.' At that time, sir, my mother and I were going to bed each night feeling guilty. After the tongue episode, Nora wouldn't open her mouth to eat and there were days when we reached the end of our tether and the dinner didn't get made. Big Lea and I moped around the house wondering what was going on with Nora, why she wouldn't eat: there must have been some purpose behind those strange things she was doing, some reason for them. She wouldn't eat, wouldn't swallow the water we gave her, just held it in her mouth or let it dribble out between her lips, forming a chain of droplets that ran down her chin. And in despair, my mother would say to her, 'Swallow, Nora, swallow! Water's for drinking, not for spitting it out.' And I'd pull her head back so she had no other option but to swallow. But, sir, I was scared, so scared of choking my sister.

And some weeks afterwards, there was the incident in the bathroom. That was much more frightening, sir.

You see, I tend to fill the tub 'cause a bath relaxes Nora, whereas when I've tried to shower her, I end up wetter than she is, sir. So I prepare a nice warm bath for her, just the way she likes it, that's comfortable for her. And I put her in carefully, sitting her on the edge of the tub and turning her, first one leg and then the other, and then slowly tipping her back so her head is almost resting against the tap, but never, never hurting her in any way. And I leave her there for five minutes, sometimes a little longer. Then I soap her up, rinse her, and say pretty things so she feels beautiful. What a belly, Nora, what a lovely belly, and such soft skin and all the freckles on your legs, what a lovely face you have; stuff like that, sir. And then comes the moment when I push her down a little, so the water covers her face, just for a few seconds, no longer than that 'cause I don't want it getting up her nose. Well, that day, when I tried to take her out after the bath, I couldn't, just couldn't. Nora made her body so stiff that it was like a heavy rock firmly moored on the bottom of the ocean – just like that, sir – or those stones in a river that can't be moved 'cause they've become embedded. Well, my sister was fixed in the bathtub and however hard I tried, I couldn't get her head out from under the water; there was just no way could I do it. And I wasn't even able to utter a word 'cause I knew my mother was going to blame me, say it was my fault. And hardly able to breathe for the shock, I felt around for the plug and pulled with all my might, pulled so hard my nails – they were softened by the water – bent back, and during those seconds it took for the water to go down the pipe, I thought my sister was killing herself, sir. I had such a fright that a few tears fell from my eyes, not many, not enough to really count as crying. But I yelled at Nora, 'What's eating you? What are you doing? What do you want?' And Nora made no noise at all: silence, nothing more than silence. After that bath, sir, when the shock had worn off a little, my sister closed her eyes and didn't open them again for forty-eight hours. And my mother burst into tears one day, looking up at the ceiling, saying, 'Come back, come back. I don't understand your daughter any longer. Come back.' She was talking to my father, sir, and I was so upset, so deeply upset that my heart shrank and that night, with Nora's eyes still closed, I said to her, 'Norita, if there's something you need, tell me. I'm staying here for you; if you weren't here, I'd leave tomorrow or the day after, but you are here and that's lucky, Nora, that's good luck. Because even if Big Lea calls you a misfortune, it's only because she's losing her nerve, because she doesn't want any of this. But if you want something, need something, let me know, make a sign, find a way to let me know, but not like this, Nora. You're killing us, killing me, Nora' And my sister opened her eyes, sir.

Those things that Nora started to do were breaking my heart. I've had little experience of suffering, sir. Nowadays, I know what it's like to think about a dead father and feel nostalgia, I know the pain of remembering, of the past, sir. I've understood time and know the past always contains a well of unhappiness. But that's all I know. I don't know about suffering, or maybe don't know enough about it. And when I watched my sister doing those things, it made me suffer 'cause what I did know was how to care for her, and if she wouldn't let me do that, then I knew nothing. After the bathtub, she seemed to be looking through us, as though we weren't there. And every time we served lunch or dinner or peeled a piece of fruit, she'd knock the knives to the floor, always near her feet. And once or twice we found her banging her head against the bedpost. Or she'd make her body so stiff it was impossible to move her, and she did that so often that we gradually stopped bringing her downstairs; we were afraid of not being able to carry her when she tensed her muscles that way. So Nora was left lying in bed and I thought that was maybe what she wanted, what she was demanding in her violent, unspoken language. Sometimes I'd lie down beside her and ask, 'Nora, don't you want to come down into the yard? Or for me to bring you some earth or read to you? I could sing to you.' Ma was all on edge and tearful, and went around the house chanting, 'Tulips, lavender, camellias, begonias, azaleas' to distract herself, sir, 'cause she didn't understand what was happening to her daughter. So there she was, chanting flower names, as though my father was with her. And I shed not a single tear, but my stomach was pumping out fire. I was trying to understand, sir, trying to understand and not resign myself to believing that the world was in fact killing itself.

I HAD A DOG THAT DIDN'T MOVE

The mayor had cancelled the August Festival 'cause for him it seemed obscene to celebrate when he was absolutely certain that the world was going to end. In town, it was rumoured that he'd prepared the basement of his house, filling it with cushions and pillows. He imagined that the world would explode into a thousand pieces, one of which would undoubtedly hit him and his family, and the very idea of his six daughters being in pain was driving him crazy. The only thing that occurred to him to prevent this tragedy was to make his basement as soft as possible.

One evening, in Javier's bar, when Catalina was admitting to me that the hatchery wasn't so bad after all – following her disappointment over Miguel, the creamery ceased to be an alternative – Marco turned up. He was late that night, sir, 'cause since the Esteban affair the Doloreses hadn't given him a moment's peace; he not only had to tend the animals, but they also required him to weed, pick the fruit, negotiate land deals, and even prepare meals for the other workers. In short, sir, they were punishing him for being a bad lot, as they put it, and that turned my stomach 'cause when it comes to bad lots, nobody comes close to that Dolores family; take what happened to my father. Anyway, Marco came in looking weary and said, 'Have you heard about the mayor?' Catalina shook her head, her eyes wide with curiosity. 'Well, he's saying that there will, definitely will be a festival the second week in September, with a band, a livestock competition and a beauty pageant.' Catalina's face lit up and Marco said that the mayor was doing it for Esteban, who'd escaped death so many times it deserved a celebration of life. After that, Marco turned to me and, in a serious tone, said, 'Lea, Lea, I've been thinking . . .' but at that moment Javier appeared and butted in, 'Lea, if you enter the beauty pageant, I'll vote for you. No one beats you for good looks.' And a silence fell between us, sir, 'cause those words didn't sound like they'd come from Javier's lips, and even his body looked odd, with his face contorted and his mouth scrunched up from the effort of getting those words out, 'cause Javier doesn't say that kind of stuff, he's more small smiles and almost invisible gestures, and I couldn't hide my surprise, though Catalina says I looked a bit suspicious too.

I sat there as mute as a marigold. Never, never in his whole life, sir, had Javier called me good-looking. I'd waited so long for that moment that I had no idea what to say; I'd always imagined that when Javier finally called me good-looking I'd be jumping for joy, I even saw myself walking down the aisle, sir, putting the seal on my life with him, but that had been a different moment, one that happened in past presents, in other years.

When I heard him, sir, I was absolutely certain that since the appearance of the foal, Javier had been making himself have feelings for me 'cause my love was easy, 'cause he knew I'd been longing for it since I was a child, and 'cause he was feeling lonely. And I started to say no, no, no way and they all thought I was saying that 'cause I wouldn't have entered that contest for all the coffee in Colombia – it isn't hard to figure out how I feel about that sort of thing – but in fact I said no 'cause my whole body was burning and that, sir, really is the end of the world. What I felt like saying to him was, 'Don't you go wanting me now that I don't want you to want me; I want to learn about love, but together we'd learn other things,' but I didn't. And Marco piped up again, 'Lea, I was trying to say that if you . . .' but Catalina butted in this time with, 'If I win the pageant this year, I'll use the prize money to have my leg operated on.'

It was the sixth time the mayor had organised a beauty pageant, sir, and every year one of his daughters won. Catalina puts her name down with the same happy smile each year, with the same hope of winning 'cause, sir, she might have a short memory but she's long on perseverance. Time and again, one of the mayor's daughters was chosen and, naturally, last year it was the turn of the youngest, who's the best looking of them all. I don't know much about beauty, and I couldn't care less whether people think I'm pretty or plain 'cause in my face there's something of my mother, something of my father, something of Grandma Jimena, and of Nora too; and my eyes are poor eyes 'cause they've always seen the same things, and my hands are dust and earth, and my legs are sturdy from going up and down the same hills, and my feet, sir, my feet are a disaster, like everyone else's in town 'cause our roads are so badly paved, it's like we've been walking on rocks.

In this town, we know nothing of beauty, but his – the mayor's – daughters have been to other places, have seen and heard, and that's given them a broader view on life, which makes them beautiful. I do believe, sir, that could be what beauty is: leaving and seeing, as happened to those girls. But the old men in town were thinking about what was under those girls' skirts and that's why they voted for them. Catalina has a sort of raw, unequal, different kind of beauty and she never received more than three votes: Javier's, Marco's and mine. I've always been against the pageant, sir, 'cause the mayor is showing his daughters the way we do our cows, but I know, feel, have an inkling that, like me, what's beautiful about those girls is their heads, and intelligence deserves better than being paraded in front of a bunch of old men who just want to get your clothes off. Every year, I say to Catalina, 'Do you by any chance have a snout, udders for milking and a tail for swiping flies?' And Catalina replies, 'Jealousy, you sow, pure, piggy jealousy.'

That evening, we smoked too much weed and when I got home I was more than half asleep. My mother said something about what Nora had done in the afternoon, but my mind was on how lovely it would be to sleep in the mayor's basement-shelter, with all those pillows. The next morning, when my mother saw me coming down-stairs, she said, 'You were well and truly out of it last night, well and truly,' and to ease the tension I said, 'Ma, don't frown. We're having a festival next week and you're going to dance with me.' 'You should be dancing with Javier. Your father used to take me out on the dance floor but nowadays I only dance with the rabbits, nobody else.' And, sir, I thought that if life was going to be like that from then on, with Nora slowly dying and my mother punishing me, I thought, let the world end this minute, bring it on.

During the following week, we all put our backs into making every corner of town look festive. The new woman helped too and, since she's an artist, she hung her painting on the housefronts. Right next to the store, she put the one I'd said I liked, with the limes in a wicker basket. And, sir, I think that was a sort of apology, but I wasn't interested in accepting apologies from someone who'd called us out in front of the whole town. I walked to her house with the painting under my arm, sweating from the heat and the effort of carrying that weight. 'I don't want this painting so close at hand,' I told her and, surprised, she let out a truly false giggle. 'Why are you laughing when you don't understand?' I asked. Her painting was back where it belonged but during the days we were preparing the town for the festival, I had to return it to Jimena's house again and again 'cause the newcomer, for some reason I can't fathom, kept leaving it by the store. One day, after so much coming and going from Jimena's house, sick of seeing the painting outside the store, I got my sister out of bed, put her over my shoulder and she lay there without going stiff or anything – the poor soul didn't care about anything by then – and I said, 'Nora, it would do you good to get outside for a while. Spending so much time in bed, you'll forget the streets of this town.' We went down the stairs as best we could, I sat her in her wheelchair, pushed my sister to the store, and parked her in the very spot where the newcomer was so set on hanging her blessed painting. Nora made no complaint, even though her knees were bruised 'cause, as we hardly ever brought her downstairs by then – we were afraid that if she moved her legs, she'd end with a knife sticking in them – I tripped and fell on the last step and cut my forehead, and Nora was bruised. But I also brought her downstairs 'cause I refused to believe that Nora didn't want to be taken out of bed, sir, and with all my heart I wanted to put an end to the lethargy we were living in.

I was untangling streamers to hang in the square when that woman turned up again with the painting. When she saw Nora – it was her first time – she stood silently observing her for a few minutes. Perhaps she noted something about Nora that made her momentarily forget what she was carrying, and the painting started to slip from under her arm. I thought it might be damaged if it fell and automatically moved save it. The newcomer's expression changed completely and she turned, still carrying the painting, and never brought it back again. That was a relief, sir, but I was intrigued by the woman's surprise when she saw my sister. Maybe Nora's gaze or her wasted body made an impression on her, or maybe she pitied her, which is the usual reaction. I don't know, but anyway, I went on untangling the streamers and said, 'Well done, Norita. Well done.'

You wouldn't believe the scolding my mother gave me for taking Nora out, sir. 'Don't you understand?' she asked, 'Can't you see that Nora's not fit to leave the house?' 'Ma,' I replied, 'Nora needs to be taken out, she has no happiness in her life. It's not like she's declared war on us.' And she retorted, 'Your sister has never known happiness and never will; she doesn't understand it, Lea. She doesn't understand happiness and we've got enough on our plates already without showing her off to the whole town in her state.' She was wrong, sir, my mother was wrong. But what could I do about it?

The mayor made the opening speech, surrounded by his troupe of daughters and his wife. It occurred to him to say something like we should feel fortunate to live where we did and to die here where we'd been raised, and you can imagine my reaction to that, sir; the only reason I didn't burst into flames was 'cause things like that only happen in movies, but I was close to it. Anyway, what started out seeming like it was going to be a festival with nothing more exciting than dancing and cows in the town square, and where the only fitting emotion was the joy of being alive, and with the chests of the townsfolk swollen with the pride of living in these four streets, seemed to go off-kilter from then on. Like I said before, in this town things come in pairs, so if Catalina falls in love, Esteban is assailed by death, and if Javier decides he's attracted to me, my sister starts doing weird things. Well, during the August Festival – we kept the name despite it being held in September – the number of things that came in pairs went on multiplying, and while some people's lives got more complicated, others found solutions to their problems.

I'd succeeded in persuading my mother that we should dress Nora in a flounced skirt and take her to the square. She'd initially said we'd have to be on our guard 'cause if Nora was throwing knives about in the living room, goodness knows what she'd do with the whole town watching, and so maybe it would be best for the three of us to stay home, with my sister in bed and us making sure she didn't get it into her head to stop breathing. The mere thought of staying in a house that was beginning to feel too big had me in a fever. Big Lea asked what we were going to say when people asked questions, wondered how they were going to look at my sister, what we'd do if she soiled herself, if she started screaming, and so on and so on. 'Ma, calm down. If any of those things happen, I'll race home with Nora, quiet her, change her, put her to bed, whatever she needs. Whatever she needs, Ma.' And she relented, sir, 'cause she felt bitter having to stay home lamenting her fate too.

So, with me pushing Nora and my mother gripping my arm like a vice, the three of us went up the hill to the square, listening to the band playing that song 'Something in your eyes drives me crazy.' And I said, 'Ma, I'm dying to dance!' Because, sir, I love dancing, just like my mother, and if Nora could, I'm certain she'd dance as well; it's my belief that things like dancing are in the genes, the desire for them is inherited. When we reached the square, I spotted Catalina, who was wearing one of her mother's midi dresses and dancing with a glass in her hand. And Marco was ordering a drink at the bar Javier had set up – he never goes to Pueblo Grande during festivals. I left my mother with Marcela and Marga, who were chatting up a storm, and Nora stayed with them. I wasn't able to see Big Lea's face when someone said, 'It truly is such a pity to see Nora this way. She should be dancing like all the other girls her age!' I didn't see her face 'cause I made the decision not to turn around, just continued walking toward Marco. 'How come you're not dancing?' I asked, and when Marco looked at me, I could tell he was already a bit tipsy, and the fragile animal he'd been over the preceding weeks was no longer there; it had gone and in its place was the raging bull with blood on its back. He said, 'You, I was waiting to see you,' and at that moment Javier appeared on the other side of the counter and puckered his lips for me to kiss and though I was embarrassed, I planted a kiss on those lips and, smiling, he poured me a drink, and when he went off to serve one of the mayor's daughters Marco said, 'Have you got one for me too?' And I burst out laughing and he ended up laughing too 'cause, sir, my laugh is like the plague: it travels a long way and is highly contagious.

While we were watching Catalina dance, Marco said, 'She's always had a thing for me,' and I replied, 'Everyone in town knows that.' 'Hey, Lea, I've been wanting to tell you that . . .' but Catalina approached looking very pleased and said to us, 'I've asked for the song that goes, "Evil, just plain evil, that's what you are, evil, just plain evil, that's your heart."' And the laughter Marco's request for a kiss had prompted exploded into guffaws at Catalina's choice. When we were heading for the centre of the square to dance, Juanita appeared dressed all in black, dark black, with her left hand clutching her breast. Catalina and I went up to her and Juanita wailed, 'Oh, your father, Catalina, your father!' And, alarmed, Catalina said, 'What's wrong, what's wrong?' thinking something serious had happened to him, but then Juanita said, 'I'm no longer Juanita! I'm back to being Juana, Julio's sister! Your father, Catalina, without so much as a second thought, your father lit a fire in me and now he's saying he isn't interested! He says he knew love once and he doesn't want me now.' And I burst out, 'Juana, the whole town loves you and not even the scrub plants like him.' And Catalina, who had taken a step back, muttered, 'If he doesn't even love me, how's he going to love you?'

And she clutched my arm and continued to me, 'I don't want my father back home.' 'Where else is he going to go, Catalina? What are we going to do with him?' 'Let him go to the forest. He can go to the woodlands,' she said. And Juana kept on with, 'Oh, Catalina! I didn't know, I thought he'd stopped, but your father's deceived me, the only thing he loved in my home was the wine. . . I don't know, I don't know! And now he's gone and set fire to my sofa!' In the distance, I suddenly spotted Catalina's father and we all watched him arriving in the square, every one of us, every single one of us with backcountry eyes.

The townswomen rushed at him and started hurling reproaches, 'We warned you, we warned you that if you laid a finger on Juana, we'd be after you, said you'd have us to deal with.' And the men surrounded Juana, with the same, 'We told you so, we told you so. That wine's a bad vintage, a bad vintage.' Catalina went up to him repeating, 'Dad, Dad, Dad,' and that made me remember I had nobody to call Dad and I noted a strange sensation in my whole body. You see, sir, I'd recalled the previous year's August Festival, when I was clapping along as my father danced to 'You know I love you, baby, so brighten my life'. And just as animals passed before my eyes whenever I saw the newcomer, this time, other images began to race past, images of my father putting a beaker of water to my lips when I was too small to hold it, and cutting the veal fillet on my plate, teaching me how plants grow, and repeating, 'Patience, Lea, you need patience in this life.' And the way my father used to look at Nora, sir, with those heavy eyes, those eyes heavy with a load of sadness, and I even remembered the words he used to say to Big Lea, 'I think Nora suffers. I honestly think Nora suffers.' And among all those memories, there appeared in my head the image of Marco saying my problem was that I didn't cry enough and, as though my eyes were a fountain, huge drops started to fall from them. Because, sir, I'll never have a father again now. I don't know if you've got one, but I don't. And I realised that there and then, while the townsfolk were soothing a broken heart and threatening an ignorant drunk. Because if my father had been there, he'd have taken my hand and said, 'My Little Lea, Javier isn't in love with you. Be patient, don't accept less.'

When I burst into tears of sorrow for the first time in months, in years, I noted a ripping sensation in my gut that wasn't flames, but grief for my life, for my dead father, for my father who was now alone, sir, without his daughters, his wife, his rabbits, his home, his town, without his life, sir. And then, in the midst of all the commotion and with the neighbours huddling around, I grabbed hold of Nora's chair and, looking her straight in the eyes, said, 'Nora, are you suffering?' And, as though she understood me, my sister opened her mouth like she did at my father's funeral and a scream hung in suspense there. It could have been caused by my tears – even I didn't know what to make of them and could only press my eyes hard to try to squeeze them back inside. Or maybe she opened her mouth that way 'cause Catalina's cry of 'Dad, Dad, Dad' made her understand that she didn't have a father either. Who knows? But at that moment I didn't want to think that her loose jaw was an affirmative, a yes, yes, I am. I'm suffering every second of the day.

I didn't have time to consider this much more 'cause, noticing the commotion, the mayor stopped the music, grabbed the mic to announce the beauty pageant, and everyone ran to try to find a seat in front of the stage. Marco and Javier sat either side of me, although Marco really wanted to remain standing and I had to command him, 'Sit down, stop drawing attention to yourself, this is Catalina's moment.' And Marco looked at me and realised how tearful I was, realised it before Javier did, sir. 'Who's made you cry? I'll kill him!' he roared, and I said, 'Lower your voice, it isn't, absolutely isn't what you're imagining.' And he repeated, 'I'll kill him,' and said it so loudly, sir, that everyone turned to look at us, and he went on saying it, with me tugging on his arm, and I could hear his mother wailing among the townsfolk, 'My son never changes, he'll never change!' The thing is that Marco thought my tears had to do with Javier and he was glaring at him with a look that said, 'I don't care if you're letting me stay in your house, I can still give you one in the snout,' and he pulled Javier up from his seat by his collar and did just that. But I've got plenty of muscle too, sir, and I grabbed the arm he'd raised for a second blow and bit until I drew blood. It was to make him see sense, to make him listen to me. He turned and I thought I was going to be the one punched, but he just put his forehead right against mine, like he did when I tried to get him out of a fight, and, in a voice so quiet hardly anybody else heard, he finally told me what he'd been trying to say for some time, 'If you want to leave, I'll help you, Lea; if it will make you happy, I'll get you out of this town full of idiots.' And then two men I knew by sight from Pueblo Grande appeared and pulled him away, and he was so drunk he let them. I don't know where they took him, sir, 'cause I turned to the people who'd helped Javier recover from his shock.

'Javier, calm it,' I said, touching his face. 'He doesn't understand, he's drunk and he doesn't know I'm crying about something else. It isn't what he thinks.' And without uttering a word, Javier nodded, sat down again, and everybody else returned to their seats. There was an air of expectancy in the crowd and the mayor was standing stock still, holding the mic. Then I noticed that Catalina was already onstage, looking down at her feet and I immediately thought she was feeling plain, and that for the first time in ages was holding back her tears. The only thing that occurred to me to ease an awkward moment was to shout, 'Catalina's the best looking'. And the townsfolk started to applaud.

Two sisters from Pueblo Grande – the grandchildren of someone who used to live in town; an elf, like you, sir, who soon realised his future wasn't here – had entered the beauty pageant. The other contestants were the mayor's sixth daughter and Catalina. Everyone was aware that the two sisters who had come onto the stage so quickly would soon be stepping down at an equal speed 'cause no one here knew anything about them, plus people preferred to either keep on the right side of the mayor or choose a local beauty; that is, Catalina. To take the edge off treating the four girls like livestock, they had to perform something they'd prepared – exactly like the cows, sir; first they show the udders to the neighbours to prove they're milkers and then they get them to moo so you can tell they're happy and well-fed. Well, the sisters did a dance routine that was downright ridiculous, but I still admired them for following the beat of the music in a way I wish I could. The mayor's daughter recited a poem almost without moving her lips, and I looked around at the townsfolk, who were murmuring their enjoyment, their pleasure, or saying they couldn't work out what she was saying but it was very sweet, and she spoke lovely. In my opinion, sir, she was a little lacking in charm, was blander than the food they give the sick. And then my klutzy Catalina planted herself in front of the microphone to sing something she'd composed herself. I haven't mentioned this, sir, but Catalina has been making up songs since she was a little girl to help get her through the days without a mother. I don't know if they're any good 'cause I don't know anything about the matter, but we're always saying to her, 'Catalina, sing to us, don't leave your songs on the page; sing them out.' And Catalina moved closer to the mic and sang a song she'd written that went, 'I've come from the corral 'cause I'm looking for love, looking for love.'

Everyone applauded except for me, sir. I believe that seeing Catalina there, where we were the only ones to think her pretty, in her manner, in her head, and seeing her hold back her tears was what made me realise that these really were my final days in town. When I saw my Klutzy, heard her singing, I was certain I'd remember all that years later, in some other place, with the nostalgia of a person who's left, never to return. 'What's up, Lea?' 'Nothing, Javier. The world's ending and the truth is, we aren't prepared for it.'

I didn't love Javier, sir. Since I was little, since he sniffed me, since even before I was born, I'd been in love with the idea of loving him and him loving me, but that isn't enough, it doesn't get you anywhere. Neither does caring for somebody. Then I recalled my father's words to my mother, 'I think Nora suffers. I honestly think Nora suffers.' And as though I'd been given a new pair of eyes, sir, eyes that were brighter, clearer, wider, I turned to look at my sister sitting in her chair, her chin almost on her chest, her hands on her lap, motionless, like when I got her out of bed. Motionless and dead, sir, 'cause though my sister was breathing, who knows how long she'd keep doing that: my sister was born dead and we've spent our lives pretending she's alive, that she has feelings.

Don't look at me that way, sir. Of course my sister has feelings, but those feelings are suffering, immeasurable suffering; she doesn't experience the world, she suffers it; she doesn't live life, she suffers it. While the towns-folk were voting for the beauties, I looked at Nora, who for me has always been the best-looking of all. And while they were crowning the mayor's sixth daughter, I whispered in her ear, 'Norita, do you throw knives around 'cause you want to die? Do you want to die?' And while everyone was clapping and Catalina was leaving the stage, wishing she had a mother to come and hug her, Nora, my sister, the woman who doesn't move, turned to look at me, sir, and she stayed like that for quite a while, looking fixedly at me, and I took her hand and scratched it a little so she'd cry the tears that needed to be shed, so she'd shed them with me, there in the square of that town she'd never been able to enjoy.

You see, sir, it feels as if everything I'm telling you happened years ago 'cause I feel old. Nineteen, and older than my dead grandmother. The world decided to kill itself yesterday, but it also died a little that day, that night. The thing is that later, when Javier had stopped serving the drunks at the bar and was dancing with Catalina, the blonde woman – the unloved, unwelcome woman, the outsider – came up to me and since I'd had a real sob – and I'm sure you know that after you've been crying you feel kind of drained but your skin is raw – I left myself open to attack, if that was her intention.

Before she could say anything – my candour isn't affected by tears – I said, 'I don't know why, but whenever I see you coming animals appear cantering inside my head.' And, uncertain if this was good or bad, she replied, 'When I see you, I see myself.' That's what she said, sir, and then she went on, 'I see you, and something about you reminds me of the girl I used to be; I was like you, I used to answer back and say things straight the way you do, but then life got more complicated.' And she said that, just as I've said it to you, just as I've always thought. While she was speaking, I was observing her the way I did that day from the backroom. I came to the conclusion that, in fact, I saw wolf packs passing when I looked at her; she was right, I saw something in her that reminded me of myself, maybe 'cause I'll be a woman like her in the future, beautiful from having seen, from having left. That's all I know. And she went on, 'Your sister reminds me of a dog I once had, a dog that was ill and couldn't move. I took it home, thinking nobody loved the poor thing as it couldn't do much besides lie there. I could care for it, make its life easier, give it love, but one day it began to inch nearer the fireplace – who knows how, 'cause it couldn't walk. Anyway, it somehow dragged itself to the heat of the fire, but each day it went closer, and I'd pull it back in case it got burned, in case it felt pain. And as I was scared 'cause my dog had stopped eating and drinking too, I took it to a friend who's a vet and she told me that it was suffering, suffering because it was living in a dead body and that was horrendous, it was like spending your whole life shut inside a narrow cardboard box with two holes to look out onto the world, but without being able to participate in it, and I saw that if I really loved that animal, that if I'd really taken it in to care for it, the only thing I could do was to end its suffering.'

I looked in astonishment at the blonde. 'What are you getting at?' I asked, less troubled now and my eyes definitely backcountry. 'Nothing, nothing at all, I'm just saying that when I saw your sister outside the store the other day, it reminded me of my dog.' I was on the point of getting to my feet to tell that blonde that the things she was saying were exactly what you'd expect from a woman without a soul, and that she was wrong, there was nothing similar about us, and what she thought she saw in me wasn't there, when my mother appeared pushing Nora's chair, saying, 'I'm going home. It's getting late and she needs changing.'

I didn't stay with Catalina and Javier until the end of the festival. After telling them I was tired, I started to make my way home. It was so dark I couldn't see much, but I managed to make out Marco in the shadows, right here on this bench where you and I are sitting. He was looking into the forest. 'I hope you aren't thinking of going in there and being swallowed by the greenery,' I said. Without replying, Marco passed me a joint and when I was about to take it, I realised, sir, that the two men who had taken him away after he'd got the wrong idea about my tears had beat him up badly and his fingers were swollen, he had a split lip, one bloodshot eye, and a very, very red face. I didn't spend long with him but had time to say that one of these days, sooner or later, I'd be leaving town. 'I know,' he said and added that if I wanted, he'd find a place for me to stay in the city by the sea. 'Get in your father's car and drive there – to the address I'll give you to begin with – and later you'll find other things, meet other people.' I didn't say anything, sir, 'cause I was tired, wasn't sure if I was awake or asleep, or if I'd been crying or not. 'They don't love us here anymore, Lea. Since that incident with Esteban, people have become distrustful, they don't wave or smile, they beat people up. The things I know would be no use anywhere else, but what you know would,' he concluded.

THE END OF THE WORLD

I'm silent for a few seconds; I need those seconds. The man looks at me and I ask if he agrees that the forest is beautiful. Don't you think the forest is beautiful? I've always been scared of it but the world ended yesterday, you see, and the forest is still here, still scary, warning us all that those who enter don't come out.

What I'm trying to explain, sir, is that if you and your dog get lost tomorrow, you won't find me here, in this town. And the reason is that my gut was burning this morning and it burns when there's a decision to be made and it hasn't been burning for a while now. It hasn't been burning 'cause I buried my urge to leave for a few months, until late October – or it could well have been early November, I'm not sure – but it was after Catalina's father had returned home and the windows were closed again and her mother's clothes put away in a suitcase; after Marco had tried every day to make peace with his parents, but they wouldn't open the door to him 'cause they didn't love him; after Javier had spent every night making coffins for the townsfolk on the mayor's orders – one for each person, sir; after Esteban had become so deeply despondent that he said, 'Death is coming and I'm here, lying on the sofa'; after Juana had brought out her brother's chair again and placed it next to her own; after I'd saved the newcomers' son when I saw him running around here one day and he very nearly went into the forest, sir, into the forest, and I warned him, 'Child, play where your parents can see you. If you're going to live here, you need to know that the forest kills, it kills.' Well, after so many things, sir, I spent weeks at home with my sister, trying to figure out what was going on inside me, and my mother said, 'Lea, my girl, get some fresh air, you're going mouldy.' Anyway, Catalina kept coming by to get me out of the house, sir, and I'd refuse, say, no, no way. And Marco left weed, chewing gum, vegetables, sobaos he'd bought in the store, and he even brought a little calf that my mother very soon had trotting home again. I didn't want to leave the house 'cause I was trying to understand, to figure out if it was true that Nora didn't want to go on living.

During the night I'd keep tally of the number of times she banged her head against the bedpost. And whenever she did, I'd run to hold and say, 'Be calm, Nora, dear. We love you here, stop wanting to leave us so soon.' My mother had started singing in the store again. And I was talking, sir, talking aloud to myself, and asking my father if Nora was suffering.

The end of the world was looming over us and people were getting more and more morbid, paying one another farewell visits and saying, 'This Christmas let's eat what we won't have when we're dead.' And I, with my thoughts focused on Nora, sir, I accepted that the world was killing itself, but was taking a whole year about it. Winter stopped being winter and became a prolonged spring, and I was surprised by how little cold seeped through the windows, 'cause around here, at this end of the map, winters mean fleece-lined collars and extra blankets, but the cold gradually disappeared and what I think now is that if the dead are cold, it's because the world is dying of heat.

One night, sir, after I'd spent the day without moving an inch from Nora's side, checking every two or three minutes to see if she'd soiled herself – my sister had stopped making that rumbling sound when she had a shit, she'd even lost any desire to feel clean – my mother found me stroking the nanny goat that was Javier's dead father and said, 'Don't be touching that goat so much, the smell will rub off on you, my love.' And I said, 'Who cares, Ma? Neither of us can smell.' Later she asked what was up with me and I answered, 'Ma, if I leave, will you come with me?' It was me asking her this time, sir, 'cause I was already thinking through what I was going to do the next day. 'We can't leave, Lea. We don't know anything else, we only know how to live here.' 'Ma, I think Nora is suffering.' And my mother started to say no, no, that wasn't so, 'Don't go behaving like your father; my Nora is radiant, my Nora is missing her father, but she'll recover soon and be her old self again.' Those were my mother's words, but I saw things differently. 'Ma, Nora is dying on us, like the world.' And without looking at me, my mother repeated, 'No, no, that isn't so. If that's what you think, go outside and get some air, so much looking at your sister has blinded you, you can't see clearly.' And she pushed me toward the door and out of the house, leaving me standing on my own doormat.

I started walking the four streets of this town in silence, in the darkness without cold. After a while I came across the blonde woman, who was coming from our small sawmill, and she asked what I was doing out so late when the town was dead at night. 'I've come outside for the wind, it's good to feel it on your face sometimes,' I replied. Since I'd stopped her son going into the forest the blonde was being more pleasant to me, and that's maybe why she said, 'Shall I be honest? Your problem is that you want to leave.' And I was silent, didn't say a word, tired of everybody telling me what my problem was. 'Your problem is that you want to leave but you don't know how because it's like you've got a dog that's suffering at home. Your life, Lea . . .' but before she could go on, I said, 'You know nothing about my life,' 'cause, sir, I was in no mood to listen to the words of an outsider I still didn't completely trust. Outsiders, sir, people from big cities, think they're smarter than everybody else but sometimes they know nothing about knowing. That's all I know.

When I returned, my mother was singing to Nora, 'Oh, love, if you leave me life, let my soul feel too.' And that night, in bed, I ruminated, sir, even more than I'm doing with you now, 'cause I understood the end of the world, understood that the world was coming to an end along with my Nora. My father used to sing that song to my sister, though only the bit that goes, 'if sorrow and life are all I have, my love, don't leave me life.' I finally understood, sir, that Nora, my soul sister, suffers the way the newcomer's dog did, and that all she wants is to die, to leave the game of life to others.

Nora wants to leave, sir, just the same as I do. I know her; I might not know about other things, but I do know

Nora. And she wants to leave 'cause there's no sense to her life, there never has been, sir, she knows the day will come when no one will be able to bear her weight, that my mother will get old and that if I stay here, my bones, my whole body, will waste away 'cause though I'm only nineteen, I look older than my mother, older than Jimena. Nora wants to die 'cause she isn't living, she's inside the cardboard box that blonde outsider described. She doesn't have life, she has death. From love, sir, she's dying from love, from love of me, from love of my mother, of my father, from love of the life we'll be able to live when she's not here. Love is a war, sir, Esteban was right: Nora is serving as a soldier in a lost war. And in war – tell me if you know more about this than I do, sir – don't soldiers kill their suffering comrades in arms? They kill them. And Nora's suffering, she's suffering, suffering.

Jimena would have done it; my mother, when she deigns to mention her mother, says she looked at Nora the way you shouldn't look at a family member. Jimena did that 'cause she knew, she knew, sir, that Nora was suffering, and she knew she'd given birth to a daughter who was incapable of freeing her own child; it was from vanity, from selfishness, but also 'cause in my family we know nothing about crying, nothing about sorrow. If Jimena had given birth to Nora, she'd have put an end to her suffering much sooner; my grandmother was like me, her most valuable asset was her head. The only thing that can fix our world, the world that starts at the door to our house and ends in our backyard and the goat, is my sister's death.

My mother has dreamy eyes, eyes that hold small dreams, small victories, 'cause I know that what my mother wants is happiness and she doesn't have any left, she's run out of it, and I know that Big Lea has a weight on her shoulders and that weight is my sister. And Nora knows that too. Helping Nora to die, sir, is helping a wounded animal to die. Don't you agree?

My older sister should have been the one to show me my path in life, that's what older sisters do, and I've always, absolutely always thought my sister couldn't do that. But Nora has shown me the way, she's said get out of here, they've stopped loving you, go, you don't need to come back, it's a wide, wide world and family is for remembering, but in life you have to move on and create a family of your own, and when the dead go, they stick around 'cause death is one day and life is many. What else am I doing here with Nora, sir, except dying? The two of us are killing each other; if I stay, we'll both die. That's why I truly believe that, though my sister is suffering, has no air, she's behaved like an older sister and has untangled my life.

THAT'S ALL I KNOW

I'm ruminating, sir, ruminating about what I'm going to do tomorrow, 'cause I've just done something that will stay with me for the rest of my life; I've just killed the world, sir. This morning, this New Year's Day that's too hot for January, just as soon as they woke, everyone started feeling their chests to check their hearts were still beating and pumping blood around their bodies, and I imagine fathers and mothers have been checking that their children still have two arms, two legs, a nose and a mouth, and Catalina will have cried during the night, and Marco will have drunk alcohol, and Javier will have hugged his foal. I slept last night, sir, slept better than I have in years. And that makes me wonder if we aren't already dead and if the death of life is just continuing to live despite the January heat. But that's all I know, sir.

If your dog were to get lost tomorrow, you wouldn't find me here in the shade. I felt my chest this morning, I put a hand to my burning gut, and I woke my sister, my darling Nora, dressed her in green – my sister looks so good in green – singing all the while. Singing while I washed her, singing while I looked at her misshapen body. I arranged her hair in two lovely braids, and carried her down to the living room on my back, slowly, without any falls this time, and our mother was still asleep 'cause she stayed up late, sir, she was awake all night, waiting for the end of the world. Before I went to bed, I said goodnight to her with these words 'Ma, cry. Your problem is you don't cry enough.'

So this morning my mother was sleeping and I slowly got Nora into her wheelchair and said, 'See what a good New Year's Morning it is. It's so sunny, so hot, the trees are so green!' And the jolting of Nora's chair as we progressed along the cobbled road stirred her dress, exactly the way Catalina makes her skirt twirl when we're pulling out the weeds from the fronts of the houses. How lovely the forest looks from here, sir. Don't you think so? With that grand canopy, its dusky colours, its immense trees. How lovely death is, like a wildflower meadow.

Has your life ever got tangled up? Well, my life has. It's got into a knot that I don't know how to untie. I'm ruminating, sir, ruminating about what to do tomorrow. Life in this town is going to be long and when your gut complains it's 'cause there's a decision to be made. And this morning, sir, I made that decision, and just like Estebitan, 'the man who was only afraid of death', I went to the edge of the forest, carrying my fear, 'cause helping my sister to die has made me face up to the fear I've borne since childhood, the greatest fear in town. And I've seen, sir, seen how the forest kills, dehydrates, empties, absorbs, swallows, 'cause it makes people so weary they die, it makes people so weary they stop believing that life will show them a path.

And I took my sister, her eyes wide, wide open but still suffering, trapped in her cardboard box, I took her to beyond the edge, just beyond the edge, and with all my strength I pushed Nora's chair into the forest. Before doing that, I settled her pretty braids on her shoulders so the end of the world would find her looking splendid. And though what I wanted to say was, 'Norita, you're going alone,' what came out in a whisper was, 'Norita, when you're able to play, I'll come looking for you.'

Then I turned and listened to the sound of Nora's chair going down the slope, deeper into the forest, the sound of the wheels moving slowly on their own, as though something – the trees or some animal I've never seen – was pushing her. I don't know about such things, sir, but I heard the wheels of the chair turning slowly and my footsteps headed very fast in the opposite direction, out of the forest, toward the life my sister has offered me, toward the years my father used to say he'd give me if he died early. And I came to sit here, sir, in the shade, not quite sure if I'm alive or dead. The world killed itself yesterday and today no one will love me. And that's all I know.

Afterwards, what's left is life, sir. After the end of the world, life is still there. And I want to go far away, and see, and become beautiful from having seen; I want to learn how to be loved and desired, allow myself to love and desire, to be loved, be desired. Like Catalina when she sang, 'I've come from the corral 'cause I'm looking for love,' I want to love, I want to love too, sir. And I carry pain and sorrow on my shoulders, like I carry Nora downstairs.

My sister isn't in the past, sir. She'll never be in the past. But I'm not sure I mind 'cause I have a clear head and when I'm a woman from somewhere else, with a daughter, and I leave flowers on the doormat, I'll say they're from her grandmother, say I don't talk to her grandmother 'cause resentments are inherited in the countryside, but she'll know nothing of that and will think that even if her grandmother doesn't love Little Lea, she does love her granddaughter, she loves her.

What am I doing, sitting here in the shade? I'm waiting, sir, waiting with you for your dog, and I'm waiting for the sound of the wood pigeons' wings flapping when my mother screams 'cause she can't find us anywhere in the house and thinks the world has killed us, has taken us from her. So that's it; I'm waiting with you for your dog, and you're keeping me company on this strange, strange afternoon.

Last night Marco left me some weed on the doormat 'cause when it comes to the end of the world, it's better not to see it, better to see something else, and I've come here to smoke it so I can stop seeing the forest and only see Nora. But I can't see her, sir; life is harsh and death is death and reality is the sorrows we don't cry over 'cause, as my father used to say, we don't belong in that part of the world that has a right to cry. And to put it bluntly, I killed my sister 'cause she couldn't do it on her own, and it would have been ill-bred and ignorant not to have done it, it would have been lacking respect and love not to act, and let them point at me, let them stare, let them stop loving me, I don't care 'cause I might not know about other things, but I do know about caring for my sister, about loving her. That's all I know. And tomorrow will be life, I want to tell the man, but I hold his gaze and say nothing. Then I look up to the sky, to its deep, deep blue and I stand up to leave.

I throw the joint to the ground. The man, who hasn't stopped looking at me, heaves a sigh, but I think he's sighing 'cause he's imagined himself going into the forest in search of his dog and dying there. I believe, I sense, that the man wants to tell me something. Lea, those who leave us stay. And I get goosebumps 'cause he's lying to me without being asked, doing it to console me, out of affection, 'cause I'm going to leave. A large dog with its tongue hanging out and a belly swollen with food appears, sniffing the air. Look, sir, here's your dog. I told you dogs weren't like me, dogs stick around.

Daunt Books

Founded in 2010, Daunt Books Publishing grew out of Daunt Books, independent booksellers with shops in London and the south of England. We publish the finest writing in English and in translation, from literary fiction – novels and short stories – to narrative non-fiction, including essays and memoirs. Our modern classics list revives authors whose work has unjustly fallen out of print. In 2020 we launched Daunt Books Originals, an imprint for bold and inventive new writing.

www.dauntbookspublishing.co.uk